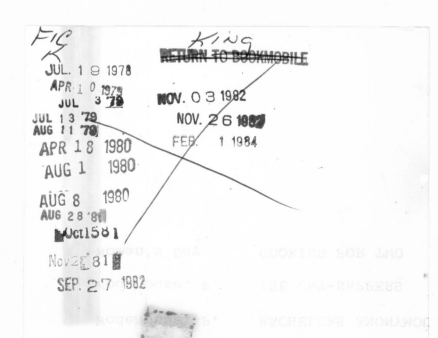

# Rage on the Range

# Rage on the Range

## DAVID KING

DOUBLEDAY & COMPANY, INC.
GARDEN CITY, NEW YORK 1977

This book is fiction and the characters are
imaginary but they are real in the sense they
are typical of the men and women who fought, and
sometimes died, to claim the West. Many of the
events portrayed are factual although some
liberty has been taken with time and place.

ISBN: 0-385-12807-X
Library of Congress Catalog Card Number 77-73332
Copyright © 1977 by Doubleday & Company, Inc.
All Rights Reserved
Printed in the United States of America
*First Edition*

*for Harriet*

# ACKNOWLEDGMENT

William H. Barton, Research Historian, Wyoming State Archives, and Henry F. Chadey, Director, Sweetwater County Historical Museum, have generously supplied background material for this novel. Acknowledgment is also made of the following helpful bibliography: "Historical Phases of the Sheep Industry in Wyoming," an address by Colonel Edward N. Wentworth, given before the Wyoming Wool Growers' Association in convention, Worland, Wyoming, August 2, 1940; *Rock Springs Miner*, Rock Springs, Wyoming, edition of March 16, 1907; *The Day of the Cattleman* by Ernest S. Osgood; *Tensleep and No Rest* by Jack R. Gage; *Wyoming Pioneer Rancher* by R. H. Burns, A. S. Gillespie and W. G. Richardson; *History of Wyoming* by T. A. Larson; *War on the Powder River* by Helena Huntington Smith; and *Encyclopedia International*, "Range Wars" by Joe B. Frantz.

David King

# Rage on the Range

◎◎◎◎◎◎◎◎◎◎◎◎◎◎

# CHAPTER I

◎◎◎◎◎◎◎◎◎◎◎◎◎◎

Handy Southern came to his senses when the gray wolf sank its fangs in his buttocks and ripped away a piece of denim and a chunk of flesh. Although so enfeebled he'd just lost consciousness, the searing pain and sight of the lobo with a hunk of him in its teeth enraged him and gave him back some strength. He hoisted the club he'd fashioned for protection at the beginning of this sorry day. The weapon was a large jagged stone bound to a stout branch with strips he'd ripped from his shirt. His blow bashed in the animal's head. The effort sapped him and he collapsed with the wolf.

The back part of Handy's head was bare white skull bone crisscrossed and clotted with dried blood. It was hammering and steaming in the sun when he revived again. He'd been bleeding from the wolf bite and the insides of his Levis were sticky. On his right side, the bandage pad he'd bunched from his kerchief was plastered to his skin like a leech but he didn't think the bullet wound was bleeding now. He swiped some of the mist from his eyes with a raw palm and pushed himself onto knees that were bare through his pants and scraped like his hands. He began to crawl once more like a turtle with a cracked shell. The club to which he clung was shoved ahead each time he moved his right arm. Slowly and painfully, he dragged his body over the old Overland Trail toward Green River.

Mangled as he was, Handy's mind was clear. Except for those times when his knees had buckled and he'd pitched unconscious on his face, everything that had happened that day was etched on his mind in sharp detail. He'd broken dry camp in a draw twelve miles east of Green River at sunup because he was hungry and dead broke. He'd sell his Winchester repeating rifle in town if he had to for food for himself and feed for his mustang.

The 1870s and 1880s had witnessed a decade of weather extremes in Wyoming Territory, blizzards and drouths, and in this parched year there wasn't enough grass on twenty acres to feed one cow. The entire country was desert. There'd been no work, not even for a top hand like him, but he'd heard they were hiring in the Green River country. He was no chuck line rider. He'd traveled across the territory from Cheyenne on a handful of beans for himself and a peck of oats for the mustang. He wanted work in a cow camp but he was willing to do anything up to dipping sheep if it would put coin in his poke and grub in his belly.

They were on him as soon as he rode out of the gully onto the flat, half a dozen whooping, rampaging Arapahos. They must have been crazy drunk because the first shot missed him and put down the horse. No Indian who was sober would shoot a horse when he could steal it. A second shot ripped through Handy's side as he fell with the mustang. He cracked the hardpan with his head and the sky went as black as a flush in spades. There had been a lot of blood from the wound and the savages must have thought he was dead. They took his saddle, war bag, Army Colt and Winchester and scalped him. The mustang was still heaving when Handy climbed back into the world. He was panting for water and gasping for air but he built the club and hammered the horse dead before he dragged himself to the trail. He'd covered his bone-bare head with his hat, which he'd found under him in a bloody slough.

At first he walked, tottering and rocking along until the weakness, pain and sun sent him to the ground. When he revived he stumbled on again. Somewhere on the trail he'd left his hat behind.

Along about noon, when his weight crumpled his knees, he started to crawl. The ground was hot as the hinges of hell and his tongue felt as thick as the heel of his boot. He put pebbles in his mouth and nearly choked to death when one slipped and stuck in his throat. It had been early morning when he'd started to haul himself over the trail. The sun was dropping toward Church Butte beyond Green River when he clawed his way to the hitch rail at Trail's End saloon in town. There he went on his face, fastened to the dirt road flat as a wet leaf. He stayed put, more dead than alive.

Even in those territorial years, Green River had a long and lusty history. The wild Mountain Men had held annual rendezvous near the town site shortly after the turn of the century. Green River had been division point and repair station for the Overland Trail stages. Now Union Pacific's steel had replaced the trail but the tinhorns and fancy women were still there. And the saloons. A dozen of them. Now it was the cattlemen and sheepmen and their hands and herders who kept the batwings swinging. It was a rip-snorting, gun-slinging, board and batten town on a rutted road and it brawled and often killed. The sheepmen, the snoozers, had put their woollies on the open range and there wasn't a cattleman or cow poke who could stand the stinkers. Especially in this dry year when the sheep cropped cow grass. Dog fights and shoot-outs between the two camps were so common nobody paid heed to a body in the street. Maybe the man had gone limp from red-eye or maybe he'd come by a load of lead.

Half a dozen waddies tromped past Handy's carcass without a second look at the shredded, sweat- and blood-caked shirt, the ripped, stained Levis that exposed raw flesh, the hairless head where flies held powwow on the skull bone.

Big Jake probably would have given the man no more attention except for the swarm of flies he scattered when he swung from the saddle and almost stepped on the head.

Big Jake was huge and said to be mean as they came. He looked more like a Mountain Man than range boss, which he was at the Lazy J eight miles northwest of town. His face was haired over with a thick black beard and his skin where it showed on his cheekbones and forehead was brown as the leaf of a crook stogie. Contained within this darkness, his eyes were fearsome. They were pale green and opaque. You couldn't see into them.

Jake started to boot the body off his trail but something about the large-boned, gaunt frame held his foot back. There was no milk of human kindness in Jake's veins but when he'd tied his horse, a buckskin standing sixteen hands and showing dark stripes below the knees and hock joints, he went back and hunkered beside the body. It smelled rotten like a corpse. Jake read sign swiftly. Indians had jumped this rider, some animal had sunk its teeth in him and he was near the end of the trail. But along the way, someone or something had paid a heavy price. A bloodied stone club lay at the man's right hand.

Jake felt the dry hot skin for a heartbeat. It was feeble. Shallow breathing was irregular. He climbed back on his heels and sized up the remains. The man's boot soles were so thin he couldn't walk over sand without burning his feet. He considered the heft of the body. Chopped up and spare as the man was, his length and breadth and size of bones showed promise of great strength. He looked as if he might be big and tough enough to wrestle with a bear when he was healthy. There was another thing to think on, a blue, unfaded path on the Levis from waist to thigh where the man had worn his gun belt low. The mark of a gunman.

Jake slung the stinking skinful of bones over his shoulder like a flour sack and lugged it down the boardwalk to Doc Bainbridge's office in the front room of his neat, white-painted frame cottage. There was a white fence around some grass that was green because the doc's wife pumped buckets of water to pour on it.

The office was small and sparsely furnished but scrubbed down. It smelled of carbolic. There was a cot at one side and Jake deposited the body on the uncovered mattress. The frail-looking, stooped, small doctor had been in the territory enough years not to be surprised at anything. His washed-out, milk-blue eyes peered over half glasses at the bloody bundle.

"He got a bad bite on his butt," Jake mentioned.

The doc rolled the man over, scowled at the gouge and felt

for a pulse. When he started ripping off the tattered shirt, Jake removed the worn-out boots and the doc shucked the stiffened Levis.

Doc Bainbridge fed the parched lips some water from a spoon. "Water's boiling on the range in back," he said over his shoulder and Big Jake brought in the kettle.

The doc scrubbed the wounds and hands and knees and body clean with lye soap and bathed the skull. He grunted some at the wolf bite and probed the side wound although Jake could see the bullet had passed through below the ribs and out the back. The odor of seared flesh filled his throat when the doc cauterized the wounds. At the touch of the burning iron the man moaned faintly but did not open his eyes or try to speak. When the doc had sheared the man's hair close, he smeared the skull with something that may have been bear grease or carbolic salve. He dressed and bandaged the side wound, salved the buttock and tied a pad on it and repeated the treatment on the hands and knees. Then he gave the darkened lips more water from a pitcher.

"Poor devil's been to hell and back," the doc told Jake when he'd rolled the man on his belly, propped his head sidewise on a pillow and adjusted the buttock pad. He covered him with a blanket. "What you aim to do with him?"

Big Jake built a smoke and struck a lucifer. "He got any chance?"

Doc Bainbridge sat behind a flat-topped desk that Jake had seen do service as an operating table. "I should say no, the condition he's in, but anybody with gravel enough in his craw to survive what he's been through today I've got to give an outside chance. Less than fifty-fifty but a fighting chance. Course he'll need constant care and careful nourishment, long bed rest, such things as salving the wounds and changing the bandage rags regularly."

"Can he travel? In a wagon. Thought I'd tote him out to the Lazy J."

Doc Bainbridge's glance over his spectacles was surprised if not downright confounded and Jake smiled inside his beard.

He knew and was proud of the reputation he bore. The doc asked, "He one of yours?"

"Nope," Jake said gruffly. "But he looks like he might have the makings."

Doc Bainbridge lifted some wrinkles to his forehead. "Ain't like you, Jake. Pick a near dead stranger from the road. Nurse him back to health. Got to warn you, it'll be a spell before he can ride or work."

Jake looked bleakly at the doctor. "Anything else?"

"Keep him out of the sun," the doc snapped, "and see he eats good. Broth at first in small amounts but often. Then soft food, eggs and porridge. Meat and vegetables when he's able to feed himself."

"I'll get the wagon," Jake said and left.

When he returned, trailing his saddle horse behind the rig from the livery stable, the doc threw a shuck mattress in the bed of the wagon. Jake bundled the man in a blanket and the doc pulled it up over his head. Jake lifted the load to the pad.

"If there's infection or fever or if he talks or acts crazy, send for me," the doc said as he turned from the wagon to return to his office.

Big Jake nodded his head slightly, and then rattled over the ruts on the road to the Lazy J. He kept thinking how hacked up the man was and how he'd fought back with a club when his gun was stolen. And the way he'd worn that gun. The Lazy J had a place for a man like that, especially when he was so down on his luck all he had to cover his skin was a borrowed blanket.

Jake turned over what would have to be done in the days and weeks ahead. The body could go on a cot in the cook-shack kitchen where Li Shu could tend him, put soup in his mouth, change the bandages and clean up when the blankets were fouled. When the gunslinger was on his feet, Jake and Jed Maine would let him know what he owed them.

The Lazy J was Jed Maine's spread. He was a dried-up old codger about as warm-blooded as a snake. He'd got that way building up his spread, fighting the Indians and rustlers and the weather. Now there was this new threat from the sheepmen who were trying to move in, spoiling the range for cattle.

Jed had three worthless sons, Roy, Rod and Ron, and a daughter, Nan. There was no place in Jed's heart for anyone but Nan and this gave Jake reason to part his beard with a grin. He'd come to the Lazy J a dozen years before as an ordinary hand. He'd made himself foreman by the overwhelming force of his strength. All Jed had seen was that the men followed him. Jake knew they obeyed him because they feared him. He had his mind set on Nan. The man who married her would get the ranch and Jake knew he could run both of them.

He was still smiling when the heavy-footed team started down the slope toward the outfit. The white house was pretty enough to make any cowboy want to hang up his rope. It was set in a grove of cottonwood trees well up from Green River, which, although only a trickle in this dry summer, showed ripples of gold in the slanting rays of the setting sun. The big barn was also painted white, and the circular corral was sturdy with horizontal logs bound with shrunk, tight rawhide to deep-set posts. There was a pasture for the horses that were being worked beyond the barn. Smoke curled from the cookhouse and the fresh, clean smell of aspen perfumed the air. At the long, low bunkhouse, also white, one of the hands was blowing a mouth organ. Some of the men were singing along. Jake thought the song was "Johnny Ringo." Right now the graze was brittle and burned but the soil was good and the grass would come back. The entire lay made Jake proud. He felt as if the ranch and Nan already belonged to him.

Jake meant to take his load directly to the cook shack but Jed was in his creaking rocker on the porch and hailed him. He ambled in an easy rolling walk to the wagon when Jake stopped.

"Who you bringing home in that condition?" Jed asked when he saw the shape under the blanket. "I thought you went to town alone."

"I did," Jake said and rolled a cigarette. He was beginning to grin again.

Jed lifted the blanket from the bandaged head. He said shortly, "He don't belong here."

"Nope," Jake agreed.

Jed screwed angry lines into his face. "What the hell you lug a corpse here for? You know him from somewhere back?"

"Nope," Jake said and climbed down. Although he loomed over Jed, he did not seem to dominate him. Jake knew Jed's formidable force and it had nothing to do with size. He was a fused stick of dynamite. "He's a down and outer," Jake told him. "His boots wasn't fit to burn." He threw back the blanket, exposing the big bandaged frame. "He's been shot and scalped and some animal has chewed on him but he had a stone club and he fought back. From the looks of his hands and knees, he's crawled a dozen miles. His lips was so dry they crackled like old paper. He ain't eaten good for a long, dry spell. He's got more guts than any man I ever saw."

Jake knew Jed was wise in the ways of the West but the chewed-up saddle tramp seemed to confound him. He asked, "You got some notion to how we can use him?"

Jake's lip curled and lifted his beard. "Yep. From his Levis, the way he'd worn his gun belt tied low on his leg, there was the mark of a gunman."

Jed's bright blue eyes got small and shiny and a tight smile dug furrows in his brittle skin. A chuckle rasped in his throat. He said, "Yep. We can use him. Providing he's properly beholden."

# CHAPTER II

Big Jake's heels clattered on the floor like snapping rifle fire when he slammed into the bunkhouse. The men recognized the sign. The harmonica stopped on a mournful note and the men scattered to the cook shack. When Big Jake was in a black mood, the only safe place was out of reach of his fists. This time he was in a blind rage. His hands were clenched as if ready to splinter the first jaw they smashed into. His beard was twitching at the left side as if his cheek were being gnawed under it, another danger signal.

At the back of the bunkhouse an aisle led to a cubicle boarded off to the side and a walled-off area across the rear. Jed's three boys occupied the big room. Jake banged into the side room. It was his office and the place where he slept. It was furnished with a cot, table, chair and a cupboard nailed to one wall. A window gave a view of the river.

Jake reached into the cupboard for a bottle of Double Stamp Bourbon and yanked out the cork. He gulped a good swallow and another. The whiskey burned his throat, threw a hitch in his stomach and made him feel meaner. He'd been the biggest jackass in Wyoming Territory to give a hand to that range bum who'd been dying on the street.

"We'll bed him in the lean-to off the kitchen here at the house until he's on his feet," Jed had decided when Jake mentioned they could make use of his kind on the Lazy J. "That way Nan can tend him."

The suggestion rocked Jake and left him almost speechless. He finally spluttered, "The cook shack's the place for him."

"Nope." Jed was stubborn when his mind was set.

"Wouldn't be healthy, having a man in the kitchen who can't get up to move his bowels. Besides, if he's got half the talents you claim for him, we need him bad. We give him the best care we can now. He pays us off when he's on his feet."

Jake was furious. He knew Jed's mind was closed like a steel trap. "But," he blustered, "the bandages got to be changed and the wounds salved."

"Nan can do it," Jed snapped.

"He's got a bite on his hinder," Jake blurted.

Jed hacked a dry laugh. "Nan's nigh twenty. She's changed her share of diapers. No difference between a man's backside and a baby's."

"There's a big difference when a man's growed up," Jake blazed. "It ain't fittin' a unmarried young lady should diaper a man."

"You saying my daughter ain't been brought up proper and knowing what is fittin'?" Jed demanded angrily.

Jake knew protest was useless but he persisted. "It ain't just that. Nan's been looking peaked and dragging her feet this past week. The task of caring for a bedridden man will tax her sorely. Her with this big house to keep, she can't stand the extra choring."

Jed glowered and said impatiently, "She's got the two squaws to do the heavy work, washing, cleaning, cooking, too, if need be."

"The Indians," Jake said hopefully. "It's them should nurse him."

"They can change the bedpans," Jed said as if that were giving in a little. "It's Nan I want caring for the man. Be good for her, give her something to do besides riding the range. Young girls need some useful things to do. Now git in there and give her a hand cleaning out the lean-to."

Jake fumed silently while he helped Nan clean out the canned goods and set up a cot for the battered stranger. He didn't trust himself to say anything but he kept looking at her whom he had considered his private property and future fortune although nothing but everyday conversation had ever passed between them. She was no longer a girl, the child he had taught to ride. She was a ripe, full-blooming woman with magnificent golden hair which she usually wore long and loose about her shoulders. Her dark brown eyes made shining crescents when she smiled which normally was often enough to give him hope. Lately, she hadn't been smiling much and her hair and eyes seemed to have lost some of their luster. She acted tired and didn't show her high spirits. She was ailing and Jed had no business weighting her shoulders with this new burden.

The activity in preparing the room for the wounded man, however, seemed to excite her for the time. There was a flush of color on her cheeks and her eyes were bright. She covered the mattress with sheets, a luxury he did not enjoy, and tucked in a white wool blanket at the foot. He carried in the unconscious man and Nan left the room while Jed and he draped the body with a nightshirt. They lay the almost weightless frame facedown on the cot with the head turned to the side on the pillow. Jed brought in a chair from the kitchen. Nan returned and moved the chair close beside the cot. She sat with her legs crossed man-fashion but hands in the lap of her Levis womanlike, looking at the white-capped head on the pillow. The cheeks were hollow and the skin pallid; it was not, Jake admitted with growing rancor, a bad face to inspect. The bones were good. The face showed strength and might be handsome when it filled out. Nan seemed interested and not at all dismayed at her charge.

"The poor dear," she murmured. "What torture he must have endured. What determination to have survived. He'll need all the care that we can give him." She looked up at Jake and for a moment her eyes were lively. "It was kind and thoughtful of you to bring him to us."

Jake was embittered and couldn't put a good face on. He stomped from the lean-to without a word. In the kitchen, he turned and glared at Jed, who had followed him. "You keep your eyes on them," he told the leathery old man. His beard didn't move because his teeth were clenched. "I don't like the

idea of a innocent girl like Nan spending her time in a bedroom with a hard case like him."

Jed's face cracked into a hundred wrinkles when he laughed.
"Man in his condition's not likely to peril anybody for quite a
spell. When he shows sign his strength has come back, we'll
move him to the bunkhouse."

Jake growled helplessly. "When it comes to changing bandages or salving," he muttered, "you call cookie or me. No need
for her to suffer that."

Jed's smile was spiteful, more a sneer. He seemed to be enjoying himself. "She can manage," he told Jake.

In his room, Jake tossed off another snort of whiskey and
pitched the empty bottle in a corner. It would be weeks, perhaps a month, before the broken-down gunman was mended
enough to be moved to the bunkhouse where he belonged and
started earning his keep. Meanwhile for hours each day Nan
would attend his needs, feed him, sit and talk with him. Because she was sorry for him and nursing him, she'd begin to
like him. He'd be grateful to her and would fall in love with
her. He'd fill out big and handsome. Jake wondered whether
the hair would grow back where the Indians had lifted it.

Jake left his room and hammered the boards with his heels.
He almost knocked over Roy, Jed's youngest son, when he
crashed out the door. Roy was a rangy, sullen-eyed, brooding
young man only a few years older than Nan. Sober, his puffy
lips were sour with the taste of the world. When he'd been
drinking, his upper lip would curl contemptuously and he'd
snarl at everyone. Right now he didn't look as if he'd been
drinking but his eyes were smoldering. Before Jake had a
chance to say a word, Roy burst out, "Who the hell's that
busted wrangler you lugged home? Pa's got Nan tending him at
the house."

Jake paused to give the remark the deliberation it deserved.
The boys were no-good scallawags but they were devoted to
their sister and overly protective where she was concerned. Jake
thought he saw a way to use them. Carefully, he said, "He's a
banged-up gunslinger."

Roy looked as if someone had belted the wind out of him. When he found his voice, he raged, "Nan, with a gunman?"

"Thought we might make use of him when he's healed," Jake said calmly.

"Maybe, but why should Pa put Nan on him?" Roy shouted. "He don't belong in the same house with her."

"I wanted to bed him in the cook shack, let Li Shu tend him," Jake said.

"That's where he belongs, not with my sister," Roy yelled. His voice was getting higher with his rising anger.

"No telling what might happen when he comes to," Jake suggested. "Wouldn't none of us want harm to come to Nan."

"That does it," Roy roared. "I'll get Ron and Rod. We'll settle this with Pa right now. We'll carry the cot and him to the cook shack. If Pa makes a fuss, we'll just kill that polecat."

Jake turned and went back into the bunkhouse. He was grinning inside his beard.

# CHAPTER III

Two storms ravaged Green River Valley with unnatural fury that night. The first broke early in the evening in the pine-wainscoted kitchen of the white house at the Lazy J. It was preceded by angry clouds that had churned up in the lean-to when Roy, Rod and Ron had thundered into the small room. Nan had been sitting there quietly in the dim light of a coal-oil lamp, listening to the wounded man's irregular breathing and watching him carefully. She was deeply concerned. When her brothers burst in, she had the stranger's head in the crook of her arm.

"What's going on here?" Ron demanded. He was the eldest, a bull of a man, hugely built, with a florid face and flaring nostrils. His eyes were brown like Nan's but they were small and had red flecks in them.

Nan was irritated at the intrusion but she said calmly, "I'm trying to force some nourishment between his lips."

"With your arm around his neck?" Rod shouted. He was the shortest of the three, no more than five feet eight, and built like a beer barrel. His arms were enormous and dangled to his knees. Rod's face was round as a full moon but deep lines dug into it from his nose to the corners of his mouth. His long nose always seemed to be pinched, as if he perpetually smelled something unpleasant.

Rod's remark roused Nan's ire and her eyes caught fire. She held a bowl of broth in her left hand, which was around the stranger's neck, and a spoon in her right. "He's unconscious," she said carefully, controlling her voice. "He's starved and has to be fed. If I don't hold up his head to make him swallow, he may strangle."

Roy's voice was surly when he said, "Let him choke."

"Please leave," Nan ordered. "He may not be conscious but loud sounds disturb him. I can feel the pulse in his neck quicken when you shout."

"Now ain't that purely painful, we should disturb him," Roy said sarcastically, but he lowered his voice. "He disturbs us. Why are you doing this, Nan? He means nothing to us."

"He needs help," she said quietly although there was turmoil in her breast.

"Where's Pa?" Ron asked.

"In his office," Nan said and slipped another spoonful of bouillon between the stranger's lips. Her hand was shaking slightly and a dribble of the soup trickled down his chin. She wiped it with a cloth.

Roy looked distastefully from the man to Nan. "What's got into Pa, leaving you alone in here with him? He's in bed and probably in night clothes. It ain't befitting."

Nan felt her heartbeat quicken. "Don't gutter-talk to me," she retorted hotly. "He's sorely hurt and sick."

"You look like you're ailing yourself," Rod said. "It's you should be in bed with somebody tending you."

Nan was tired and her bones ached but she stiffened and sat upright. "I'm quite well, thank you," she said remotely.

"Why'd Jake carry home this tore-up drifter?" Ron asked. "He should of left him on the street to die."

"Don't fault Jake," Roy said. "He's got a job in mind for the man to do if he comes 'round. Jake meant to put him in the cook shack. It was Pa set him here and wouldn't let nobody excepting Nan look after him."

Rod sniffed disagreeably and said, "Pa's old. His mind is soft. Time is come for us to do something. We got to for the sake of Nan. I'll tote him to the cook shack. You two can carry the cot."

Nan was alarmed. "No," she cried. "It would kill him to move him."

Jed abruptly loomed in the doorway. He was shorter than Rod but he seemed to dwarf them all. Nan was frightened, not for herself but for the boys. She could feel her father's wrath and see it in the blue ice of his eyes. "What the hell you three doing in this sickroom?" he roared. He never swore in front of Nan.

Roy sneered but his voice was respectful when he answered. "We're fixing to move that critter you took in to the cook shack. Nan's sick."

Jed turned quickly to her and concern replaced the ire in his voice. "What's wrong, Nan? If you ain't up to it, I'll get the squaws."

Nan was incensed. "I feel fine," she flared. "Of course I can do whatever is needed. I want to." Suddenly she was inflamed and said tensely, "It's the boys who make me sick. They and their accusations. They think it's immoral I should care for this man."

"They been pestering you!" Jed declared to Nan but accused the brothers.

Nan was silent.

Ron snorted and said loudly, "She don't belong here with the likes of him."

On Nan's arm, the wounded man turned his head and parted his lips as if to speak. Then he lapsed back into his coma.

"Git into the kitchen," Jed commanded brusquely. "You're fretting him." He turned to Nan. "You come, too. Turn down the lamp so it don't shine in his eyes if he wakes."

Nan knew her father was very angry. In the kitchen, he sternly pointed to chairs about a round table in the middle of the room. A lamp burned on it, puddling a red- and white-checked cloth with yellow light and casting hulking shadows against the walls. The big room was warm and still smelled yeasty from baking. The three sulky young men sat on one side of the table facing Nan and Jed on the other.

Nan was breathless, partly from the air that seemed oppressively still, and partly from being included in this confrontation. When Pa had something to say to the boys, he usually had his word privately with them in the office.

Jed glared at his sons. "You have no business in the lean-to," he told them.

"Much as her and more'n him," Roy said and looked toward the closed door to the shed.

Jed's eyes frosted. "Coyotes!" he called scornfully. "Brainless animals. Go out and bay at the moon. What the hell you doing here? That man in there looks to be mortal wounded. We're doing what we can to save him. You roused him maybe to his death. What you doing here?"

"We come for Nan's sake," Rod mumbled.

"How you figure it like that?" Jed asked angrily. "What the tarnation hell you think the worthless three of you could help her and what for?"

"We come to save her," Ron said defiantly.

"Save her from what?" Jed demanded. "I put her in there with the stranger to see he didn't die. There's nothing here she needs to be saved of."

"Maybe save her from herself," Ron muttered. "She don't know men or how they're like. When we come in she had her arm around his neck like a woman anybody can buy."

Nan blinked away the angry tears that filled her eyes. Her voice caught when she said, "I told them, Pa, I had raised his head to try to get some broth between his lips."

Jed was on his feet filling his lungs with wrath. There was thunder in his voice and lightning in his eyes when he roared at Ron. "Mind your tongue. What you said should never be said of any lady and most of all your own sister. You make the air stink with your barnyard talk. You are not fit for her company. None of you are sons of mine but studded by Satan." He looked down at Nan. She had tried to hold back her tears but she was weeping bitterly. Gently, he said, "I am sorry. Words you never should of heard have been said. Now you know your brothers for what they are. Drunkards. Womanizers. Go back. They won't foul you again."

Nan's back was straight but it was trembling when she left

the kitchen. She was agitated and angry and hurt at what her brothers had said and done. She had heard how they caroused in town and knew how they upset her Pa. He had done a Christian kindness to take the mutilated man into his house. The boys had been an intolerable burden to him, and now she was frightened at what he might do to them for talking back the way they had and saying she was cheap and wrong. Pa had an awesome temper.

The stranger was sleeping fitfully when she took her place beside him. His head jerked on the pillow and she thought he moaned weakly. She did not know whether this was good and a sign he might be regaining consciousness or an indication he was worsening. She dribbled water on his dry lips and impulsively reached to stroke his wrist above the bandaged hand. The skin was dry and brittle. It felt hot and the arm bones were sharp. She knew nothing of him except that he was a brave man who had suffered and her heart hurt for him.

Through the flimsy door that separated the lean-to from the kitchen, she heard her father raging at her brothers and they ranting back at him. The low ceiling of the small room and the narrow walls seemed to be pushing in on her as she shuddered at the hateful words they shouted at each other.

Pa's voice was strident. He told the boys, "You've not done a lick of work in all your life. I'm shet of you."

"What you aim to do, Pa?" Roy asked mockingly.

"Git out," Pa blazed. "You git no more of me. I cut you off. I'm sending the lot of you packing. I never want to see you on this range again."

"You can't do it, Pa," Rod said confidently.

"We'll not leave," Ron said. "We'll stay right here on land that's going to be ours. You put us in the bunkhouse but we're not going any farther."

"You can't put us off or cut us off," Roy said. "It was Ma's dying wish you take care of us and you promised her."

"First you smirch your sister and now your dead Ma," Jed yelled but his voice cracked. "Stay in the bunkhouse if the hands can stand the smell and sight of you but keep out of my house and away from Nan."

Taunting and assured, Roy said, "We got our rights. We'll do what we want and you'll foot the bills to save your name and face. We'll see Nan whenever we damn please and you'll not come between us."

At this moment, before Jed could reply, the second storm that night broke over Green River Valley. There was a blinding streak of lightning and a shattering crash of thunder that rolled over the Salt River range and down from the Tetons. It rumbled over the high arid plateau and echoed in the canyons. The first mighty clap shook the lamp on the kitchen table. It was followed by a moment of dead calm before thunder again slapped the land. A spattering of rain rattled on the roof.

"Rain!" Jed cried.

It washed away all argument and angry words.

Wind that had swept full-bellied Pacific clouds into the Rockies blew itself into a gale. The valley was whipped with sheets of rain.

"We're saved," Ron exulted.

"We're not going under," Rod exclaimed.

"It's come in time," Roy shouted.

Glorying in the torrents of rain that clattered on the lean-to, Nan wondered at the change that had come over her brothers. It was almost as if they cared about the ranch. They were sitting in silence in the kitchen thinking, she knew, only of the moisture for the burned-out graze, water for the thirsty herds. Nothing else mattered. The silence seemed to say to her that each was drenching himself, feeling in himself grass roots springing into life. It had been the drouth, she told herself, the misery of the parched land, the galling taste of dust that had brought Pa and her brothers to each other's throats.

"This is a drencher," she heard her father say when, after half an hour, the downpour continued without a letup.

"We can use every drop of it," she heard Roy say. She thought he sounded happy.

"Wonder what it's like upstream?" her father said. Nan was puzzled. He sounded worried.

"Hope they're lucky as us," Ron said.

"It's too much, too fast." Her father's voice was nervous. "The ground is baked. The earth is so hard-caked, it can't soak in the water."

"If it keeps up, it'll run off into the draws and gulches," Rod said lightly. "We'll have a water hole in every gully."

"If they're getting it upstream," her father said tightly, "there'll be a flash flood. The cattle, they'll be in those draws or near the river, wherever there's moisture enough for grass."

"If it keeps up," Roy said, "we'll lose the herd."

"We'll lose the ranch without the cows," Ron said gloomily.

"We'd be busted," Rod said.

Unhappily, Nan thought she understood the sudden change in the attitude of the boys at the beginning of the storm. The rain would save the ranch. Without the herds, the boys would have to work. Her father must have felt it, too, because when there was no lessening in the cascading storm, he said gruffly, "Go check the river, Roy."

Roy did not reply, but after a moment Nan heard the back door pushed open and slam back. The others in the kitchen waited without speaking until he came back. She heard him put down a lantern and shake his slicker.

"Green River is over its banks," he announced. His voice was brittle. "From the sound of it, there's a wall of water coming down the valley."

"That means the draws are full," Nan's father barked. "We'll have to ride out, all of us. Every man child. Through every gully and along the riverbank. Drive the cows to higher ground. Rope the ones that are mired. Ron, get down to the bunkhouse. Have Jake whip up every poke we've got. No telling how long we'll be out. Tell them to bring what they'll need for three, four days. Rod, wake up Li Shu, tell him to lay out traveling grub for the saddlebags. Roy, you come to the barn with me."

Nan heard her father's quick heels rap to the back door

where she knew he always hung his slicker. She did not hear Roy's footsteps. Roy said, "You going, too, Pa?"

"I said every man we can muster," Nan's father snapped.

"Him?" Nan knew Roy was pointing to the lean-to door.

Her father's voice sounded scornful when he said, "He couldn't ride a nightmare in his condition. Come on, now."

"I ain't going to budge," Roy answered stubbornly. "Him alone here, in that room with Nan. I ain't going to go. I'll stay and watch out for things."

Nan choked back an angry outcry as she heard her father say, "We been over that. Move."

She heard a chair push back and Roy said, "All right, Pa, but if we come back and he's harmed her, or even changed her way of thinking, I'm going to kill him."

◎◎◎◎◎◎◎◎◎◎◎◎◎

# CHAPTER IV

◎◎◎◎◎◎◎◎◎◎◎◎◎◎

Above the lashing fury of the howling storm, Nan heard the protesting neighs and snorts of the horses as the cursing men of the Lazy J rode off in the blindness of the night to round up whatever cattle they could find. The house, the entire ranch suddenly felt empty. She and the wounded stranger occupied the place alone in the fragile lean-to. The Indian women, Full Moon and Running Doe, slept in their own quarters in a shed beyond the white house. Li Shu had his cot in a room off the cook-shack kitchen. Nan was not afraid. Her only concern was for the condition of the man with whom she sat so intimately.

She wondered again, as she had during the hours he'd been in her care, who he was and what he was and how he'd come to his sorry state. His face was well boned but hollow-cheeked and looked drained of blood. Above the blanket, she felt his arm and back. He was all bone with no flesh upon him, as if he had not eaten for a month, and she spooned more broth between the dry, dark lips. He opened his eyes. Above the cheekbones in his gaunt face, they seemed enormous. They were as blue as the big sky. He seemed to be looking deep into her and he murmured something. She bent close to hear his words, learn his wants.

"Emma," he whispered, staring at her. "Thank God. I thought . . ." His eyes closed, shutting her face from his mind, and his faint voice trailed away.

She waited intently but his lids remained shut and he spoke no more. She felt his pulse and put her palm close to his nostrils to feel his breathing. He was back in his coma but he still lived. Emma? She asked herself, who was Emma? A wife he'd left behind? The thought troubled her. She did not know this man or anything about him except that he was courageous and in need of help but she did not want him to have a wife. The reaction she admitted to herself shocked and puzzled her.

She dozed in the hard, straight chair in the dimly lighted, shack-like room with the torrents of rain pounding on the roof. Now and then, when her head dropped, she awakened and felt keenly aware of her responsibility. Each time, she felt his wavering pulse and placed another spoon of water between his lips. Then she would fall asleep again in the flimsy shack that seemed to have become a secure refuge, a small shelter on an island where the stranger and she were safe.

Throaty gasping startled her to wakefulness. Frightened, she felt the man's forehead. Although the storm had chilled the room, his face was wet with perspiration. Under the blanket, she felt his nightshirt. It, too, was wet and under it his body felt warm. He opened his eyes and they were bright with fever. He closed them almost at once. She hurried to the chest in the hall for another blanket, which she wrapped snugly about him, and then went to the kitchen for a bowl of water and a towel. She sat patiently bathing the perspiration that welled on his forehead and temples and streamed down his cheeks until the wet, gray light of the dusky dawn filtered into the lean-to and she heard the Indian women come into the kitchen.

"Full Moon," she called softly. It was an effort to speak. She was very tired and her chest hurt when she breathed. "Full Moon, come in here."

Nan heard the squaw padding across the kitchen with maddeningly slow deliberateness. When she opened the lean-to door, she was still wrapped in a red cotton blanket that was soaked. Her long black braids were dripping. The wet blanket made her seem more squat and plump than usual. Her nose was squashed into a full, round face. She regarded the bandaged man on the cot with indifferent dark eyes.

"Heat the kettle of broth," Nan told her. "Then come in and sit beside him. Every now and then put a spoon of soup between his lips. Give him water the same way. Wipe the per-

spiration from his face with a damp towel. See that he remains
fully covered. He is burning with fever. I am going to town for
the doctor."

For the first time, the Indian woman's eyes showed interest.
"You cannot," she said flatly. "Water runs like a river on the
trail. Your pony would go down in the mud."

"I must get the doctor," Nan said firmly. "And you'd best
get out of that blanket or you'll need him too."

Full Moon grunted. "Send Li Shu."

Nan stood and said impatiently, "You know he does not
ride."

"He can take a wagon."

"A wagon would mire more quickly than a horse," Nan said
irritably. "Now do as I say. There is no time to argue."

Full Moon shrugged and returned to the kitchen. Nan
thought it must have been the longest conversation she'd ever
had with the Indian woman. When Nan bent over the cot to
towel the face again, she felt faint and grasped the chair for
support. In a moment the dizziness passed and she stepped
into the kitchen. Full Moon had draped her blanket over a
rope behind the range next to Running Doe's wrapper. Running Doe must have overheard the conversation in the lean-to
because she'd built up the fire and had the coffeepot beside the
soup kettle on the stove.

"Ready soon," she said, pointing to the pot. She was young,
lithe and pretty, and her eyes were lively.

"I don't have time," Nan said and went upstairs to her bedroom. Hastily, she pulled on a heavy man's shirt, Levis and
boots. When she leaned over to tug at the boots, the faintness
returned. She took a poncho and broad-brimmed hat with her
to the kitchen. Full Moon had gone to the lean-to and Running Doe had poured a cup of coffee. Nan hesitated and sat at
the table. She needed the coffee.

Through the window above the tin sink, the morning was
dismal and the rain was still slashing the valley from the northwest. The range was quickly warming the kitchen and drying
out the dampness. Nan opened the lean-to door and propped a

chair against it. Full Moon was wiping the stranger's face. Under the blankets, his ribs scarcely moved when he breathed.

"Leave the door open," Nan told Full Moon. "I had not noticed how cold and moist the air is."

Full Moon turned resentfully to the cot. "You stay," she told Nan. "He die anyway."

"No!" Nan's stomach felt hollow, at the words or from hunger and exhaustion. "I must hurry."

She wove her golden hair into a knot and pinned it atop her head while she gulped the coffee. With the flat-topped black hat clapped low on her forehead and the poncho covering her shoulders-to-knees, she sloshed across the puddled yard to the barn. The wind buffeted and the rain pelted her. Little Sister, her brown and white pinto, recognized her step and whinnied before she reached its stall. The paint nuzzled under her arm while she bridled and saddled it.

"Little Sister," she told the pony, taking a moment to rub its nose, "it's not the kind of day for our usual ride and we aren't going to like it."

At the door, the pony shied at the driving storm but put its head down when Nan leaned over its neck and urged. Little Sister stepped warily up the wagon trail through frothing dirty streams. Although her mission was urgent, Nan gave the paint its head and let it pick its way. The footing was greasy under the running water and the horse was uncertain. Twice it slipped and stumbled and Nan pulled it to a halt before it went to its knees. At the top of the hill, the road to Green River leveled out but still Nan did not dare lift the pony over a walk because she feared hidden sinkholes and ruts.

Nan was drenched and shaking with the cold rain and fatigue. Aches stabbed her body and chest but she pushed on. She was determined the stranger should not die. Her thoughts were only for him. She knew her concern should extend to her brothers and father, struggling in the storm-whipped valley to salvage the remnants of the herd. Especially Pa. He was beset by problems. The drouth had plagued him all summer. The boys had vexed him. The sheep that were devouring the sparse graze obsessed him. Now this storm that ravaged the land. But it was the stranger in the lean-to who filled her feelings and mind. Her heart ached for him. He was helpless.

The ride to Green River ordinarily took less than one hour. It took Nan more than two but the wind and rain were diminishing as they neared the edge of town. In relief, Nan shook Little Sister out of its walk. The pony stumbled and went down, throwing Nan in a deep pool. Little Sister was not hurt and pawed to its feet but Nan had twisted her ankle in the stirrup. It throbbed with pain and she had trouble hobbling to the horse and remounting. She was drenched and all of her clothing clung to her skin and chilled her. The pony slogged down the crested main street where lights were burning in many of the buildings but no one was on the street. Dr. Bainbridge's trim white cottage looked dirty and gray in the drizzly early morning but a lamp was lighted in his office window when she tied up.

"Nan!" he exclaimed when he answered her rattle at his door. Although it was early, he was shaved and dressed. "Come in. What happened?"

She limped into his office and he snatched a blanket from the cot. "Here. Go into the kitchen by the stove. Get out of your wet clothes. There are towels in the cupboard. Dry yourself and wrap up."

"It's the stranger," she gasped, steadying herself at a corner of the doctor's table-like desk. "He . . ."

"Not yet," the doctor interrupted. "No talk now. First we attend to you."

Nan nodded her head and obeyed with a feeble smile. She was quaking as she dropped her hat, poncho and soaked clothing beside the warm range. Her right ankle was wrenched with pain that reached her stomach when she struggled with that sodden Justin. She scrubbed her skin with a rough towel she found in the cabinet and wrapped the blanket tightly about her.

"It's the stranger Jake brought in last night," she began

when she stepped back into the office favoring her right foot. Her teeth were chattering.

Dr. Bainbridge stopped her again. He looked as if he were trying to make his face stern but it was lined with worry. "Not yet," he said. "Don't try to talk yet." He went to the kitchen where she saw him pour brandy in a cup before he filled it with steaming black coffee. "Drink this first," he told her when he gave her the cup. He watched her closely over the tops of his half glasses as she took the cup in both hands and sipped. The laced coffee warmed her stomach and she smiled gratefully at him.

"What's wrong with your foot?" he asked when the cup was nearly empty.

"It's not my foot I came about," she cried. "I twisted it in the stirrup. It's the wounded man Jake brought to you last night. He has a high fever. He was delirious. He slipped back into a coma. I don't know. I think his wounds have infected."

"Let me see your foot," the doc demanded. He knelt before her, running his fingers over the foot and ankle. "No broken bones, but it's hot and swelling. We'll salve and bandage it. That should give you some relief." He pushed to his feet and started for his medicine cabinet on the wall behind his desk.

"The stranger," Nan groaned. She felt helpless.

"Why didn't you send one of your men?" the doctor asked sharply as he anointed the ankle and started swiftly to bandage it and the foot.

"There's no one at the ranch," she said wearily, leaning back against the wall and closing her eyes. "When it started to rain so hard, they all went out to round up the cattle and drive them to higher ground. They were afraid they would drown. Even Pa went. There's only the Indian women and Li Shu and me on the place. I couldn't send any of them."

"So you came for me through the storm." Dr. Bainbridge studied her a moment and his face, which could be stoical as an Indian's, seemed kind and gentle. He said quietly, "It was a brave thing to do." He stood. "I'll go right away. You say high fever and delirious. Anything else?"

"His breathing is shallow, pulse irregular." Nan got to her feet clutching the blanket. "Do you think Mrs. Bainbridge could find me some dry clothes?"

The doctor chuckled. "Mrs. Bainbridge can bundle you up and tuck you in bed."

Nan shook her head stubbornly. "I'm going with you. You may need me."

The doctor looked closely at her and hesitated. Abruptly, he said, "All right. At least I can keep my eye on you out there. I'll have Mrs. Bainbridge put you in some warm clothes. We'll go back in my buggy. That will give us some protection."

"My pony," she said, almost in a whisper. She was wretched with weariness.

"We'll leave her at the livery, have Adam give her a good rubdown, feed and water and watch her. Jake has a wagon from the stable. He can ride her back when he returns it."

The storm had passed, the rain had stopped when they started back to the ranch but it was a dark morning soaked with an overflowing of moisture that seemed to lie in layers above the earth. Dr. Bainbridge had wrapped a woolen blanket that smelled of camphor over the dress and heavy underclothing Mrs. Bainbridge had provided and hooded her head with it. Nan had left her soaked clothes and boots behind and wore a thick pair of the doctor's socks inside a pair of his moccasins. Warmed by the clothing, the brandy and coffee and spent by the long night's vigil and the punishing ride to town, Nan soon was asleep. When she awakened, they were skidding down the hill to the ranch house. She was not rested from her sleep.

There were no horses in the corral or in the barn where they left the doctor's rig so Nan knew the men had not returned. She called out Li Shu to care for the doctor's horse and waded across to the welcome warmth of the kitchen.

Running Doe turned from the stove. A smile brightened her dusky face. "I fix hot breakfast," she said.

"Then it's into bed for you, young lady," Dr. Bainbridge told Nan. "You've had a rough time."

Nan left her blanket on a kitchen chair and walked to the
lean-to on the toes of her right foot. Full Moon observed her
clothing and stiff gait.

"I say no good you go," she told Nan. Her black eyes looked
angry.

"Is he all right?" Nan asked quickly. She could not see
whether the stranger was breathing.

"He still live," Full Moon said, "but now you sick." She re-
linquished the chair to the doctor.

Dr. Bainbridge squinted at the man on the cot and frowned.
He took the patient's pulse, felt his face and slipped his hand
under the blankets for the heartbeat and body temperature. To
Nan he said, "It's fever. I'll get some laudanum and belladonna
into him and then I'll remove the bandages and check for infection. Do you have some brandy in the house?"

Nan nodded tiredly. "Will he be all right?"

The doctor was not reassuring. "You've done more than you
should. I'll do all I can. Now take a large spoonful of brandy in
a cup of hot coffee. I don't want you to wait for breakfast. Get
yourself right into bed with lots of covers. Sleep. Don't get out
of bed until I tell you to get up."

Nan looked at the feverish man on the bed. She thought his
cheeks had sunken since she'd left. Her breath trembled in
her chest. "But . . ." she started to protest.

"If I need anything, I'll ask the Indians," the doctor said
sternly. "Do as I ordered."

Nan smiled wanly. "I don't have the strength to argue. But
if there's any change—" her breath caught in her throat—
"either way, please let me know."

She limped from the lean-to.

Above his glasses, Dr. Bainbridge watched Nan. She disturbed him. There were no outward symptoms of anything except exhaustion, but her prolonged exposure to the cold rain
and the tiring ride made him uneasy. For the moment, he'd
prescribed what he thought she needed most. Rest and
warmth. But he could not be certain.

For the next two hours Dr. Bainbridge devoted his attention to the weakened, wounded body. There was no doubt the man was near death. He surely would have died before the day was done, the doctor thought, had not Nan risked her own life to come for him. He still was not sure that he could save him.

The doctor worked methodically, first removing the damp nightshirt and covering the patient with blankets where he could as he removed the bandages. The wounds were clean and had not festered but the skin over the man's entire body was very hot. The doctor called Full Moon to help and bathed the body in a solution of lime and sulphur before treating the wounds with carbolic salve and rebandaging them. He decided not to cover the skull as before. He salved the bone and protected it with a loose pad of bandage rags. The fever, he thought, had resulted from long exposure of the bare bone to the sun. He could only hope there was no permanent brain damage.

Full Moon brought a flannel nightshirt and fresh sheets. When the man was again under the blankets, Full Moon held his head up while the doctor spooned Dover's Powder dissolved in water into his mouth. Dr. Bainbridge left Full Moon with instructions to swab the man's face from time to time with a towel dampened in a bowl of lime and sulphur water.

Dr. Eli Bainbridge was not a young man. He was nearly fifty years old, thin and gray as an old fence post from too many years of rough buggy rides to remote ranches through blazing summer heat and winter blizzards. He'd treated too many gunshot wounds, splinted too many arms and amputated too many legs. He'd delivered too many skinny babies and seen too many of them grow up only to reach boot hill. Now he was tired from the treacherous drive to the Lazy J and the tense minutes he'd spent with the patient. He declined the breakfast Running Doe offered but took a cup of coffee at the table in the kitchen before going to Nan.

He'd done all he could for the patient, everything within his capabilities. He distrusted Dover's Powder as a treatment. It was a commercial concoction of opium, ipecac and sugar of milk. Physicians resorted to it for every malady but Dr. Bainbridge did not hold with prepared drugs. The opium, however, was a sedative and should make the patient more comfortable and induce sleep.

He thought Full Moon's expressionless dark face had tightened and blanched when she'd recognized the nature of the scalp wound. Where in hell had she thought the braves had come by those coveted trophies? It was grim justice that a squaw should nurse this man.

What manner of man was he? The doctor was frankly puzzled at the care and attention Jed and Jake were giving him. Neither of them was a good Samaritan or even thoughtful. They'd left Nan without a hand to help. It bothered him to think of the demands they'd make upon the patient, should he recover.

Nan was not asleep when he went into her bedroom. Her face was flushed and under the covers she was shaking with chill. Her breathing was erratic. She seemed to gasp for air. She coughed frequently, raising a rust-colored, pus-laden sputum.

Dr. Bainbridge was agitated. These were the symptoms of lung fever, pneumonia. Frequently it was fatal.

◎◎◎◎◎◎◎◎◎◎◎◎◎◎

# CHAPTER V

◎◎◎◎◎◎◎◎◎◎◎◎◎◎

Jed was an exhausted and outraged old man when he and his hands drove toward high ground from the roaring river in the bleary bleakness of dawn with some one hundred head of cattle. He had built his spread and herd over a quarter of a century with nothing but toil and sweat. Now one night had washed him out.

With Big Jake, a dozen hands and his three sons, Jed had labored blindly in the raging blackness to move the cows from the rushing water. He and the hands had strung out tail to nose with the horses plodding through a torrent up to their hocks. The men whooped to keep in contact as much as to move the cattle. When Jed felt they had a bunch, he'd shout, "Now turn them!" and the order would pass on down the line. When the horses pawed out of the stream, some cows plodded on before them but others had to be pushed or rope-whipped to start them toward solid ground. When they had a bunch collected well up from the river, the sodden crew would return to start all over again.

Jed swore and drove the men as relentlessly as he did himself. It was more than a man should be called upon to tolerate, he thought bitterly as he fought to lead his men safely upstream and save what cows they could. Damned sheepmen and their stinkers, burned-out range, now more rain in one night than they'd had all year. He wouldn't let them beat him, by God! he wouldn't. He knew he was old, nearly sixty, but he'd done it before. This was the worst cattle drive he'd ever known but give him a small herd and he'd do it again.

Somewhere behind, a cow or horse stumbled and fell. It

wasn't so much that Jed heard the sound above the thunder of
the river as he felt the falter in the line before the word
reached him, "Man down!" Jed halted and called the roster of
his men. The names crossed and Jed got back the answer before he was halfway through. It had been Roy. He was up on
his horse again.

"Damn it!" Jed roared. "Pass the word. Anyone goes down
again, we don't stop to pick him up."

Throughout the night, while the storm haggled the land,
they battled the river and the cattle. When the wind and rain
thinned with the watery gray of dawn, they rounded up the
cows strung in bunches away from the river, one hundred head,
and drove them upland to the pitiful handful they'd rescued so
far. The drouth already had reduced the herd to a thousand
head. They'd work on upstream and search each draw and
gully. He'd be lucky, Jed thought, if he could throw together
five hundred head but that wouldn't be the complete disaster
he'd feared. A sorry sight, a hundred head of scrawny longhorn
moving restlessly, but there'd be more below. And in the draws,
carcasses, but others standing shank-deep in the muck. It was
enough to make any man worth his keep sick to the bottom of
his stomach but it wasn't as bad as it might have been.

Jed was riding point, leading the herd to a small mound far
back from the river and the draws when Jake rode up. Water
was dripping from the matted bush of his beard and his eyes
were opaque.

"Better take a look at Roy's horse when you get a chance,"
Jed told him. "Any idea how it come to take that fall? Slip or
stumble on a stone?"

Jake's eyes flashed angrily. "Horse didn't fall. Roy did. Fell
out of the saddle."

"What the hell," Jed blazed. "Roy's a good rider. Only thing
he *can* do good. Chew it finer, Jake."

"Roy was drunk," Jake growled.

Inwardly Jed fumed but he kept his voice level. "I know you
got no use for the boys, Jake. Don't fault you on that. But

that's no reason to prattle tales that can't be so. Roy left the house with me. He was mean but he was sober."

"Took a bottle with him," Jake said and his beard jumped as his face twitched. "Told him to leave it behind."

"Took a bottle when he knew what we was in for!" Jed was furious. "Send him to me when we got the cows bunched on that hill."

"Sure." Jed thought Jake's eyes gleamed. "The men can't take no more, Jed. They're plumb tuckered. They got to eat and rest."

Jed himself felt that if he ever climbed down from the saddle, he'd never be able to get up again. He was at least twice the age of most of them but he sat straight and barked, "There's still nine hundred head, maybe on the river, maybe dead in the draws, hopeful up on the range. We don't stop until we've got every cow is still afoot."

"We got to pull up awhile," Jake said explosively. "Stop a spell to eat and build a smoke."

"They got jerky and biscuits," Jed said shortly. "They can eat and smoke in the saddle."

Jake glowered. "It's been one hell of a night. They won't take it. Not if we're going on up the river, work the draws with water belly high. Not if we're going to the range. Maybe we'll be out a week. The men got to have coffee and hot food and get some sleep."

Jed's belly churned when he thought of the time they'd lose but he knew Jake was right. The horses as well as the men needed feed and rest. "All right," he finally agreed. "When we get the herd on the hill, we'll make camp. Send one of the hands back to headquarters. Have him load up a wagon. Have Li Shu boil up a big pot of Arbuckle's and have your man bring out a bag of coffee and a bag of flour. Beans and sowbelly. All the biscuits the Chinaman has got. Fresh meat and potatoes. Whatever hot Li Shu is fixing up for today that we can warm over. Get feed for the horses, dry wood and blankets. Whatever he can lay his hands on. There'll be no going back for another load. We're going to stay out until we've rounded up every cow

and dogie that still breathes. Right now, the men can eat
what they've got and stretch out until the wagon gets here.
Then we'll have coffee and a hot dinner and then we'll work
until the sun is down, if ever we get to see the sun again."

"Fair enough, Jed," Jake said. Jed thought his eyes went flat
with cunning. "The boys will like that. I'll go back myself for
the supplies."

"The hell you will! You need your rest more than anybody.
Send the least of the men."

"Somebody ought to check on Nan," Jake muttered resentfully. "See she's all right."

Jed snorted. "Won't do, Jake. You stay put. Nan's capable.
Whoever you send, tell him to stay away from the house.
Don't want nobody nosing around."

Jake didn't answer. He reined his horse about and Jed called
after him, "Don't forget, send Roy to me."

A clump of cottonwood trees shed water from their dry
leaves on the far side of the knoll where Jed's band gathered
the small herd of puny cattle. The cows were so exhausted
from the rushing river and the driving wind and rain, they
didn't mill or bawl but stood where they were stopped looking
dumbly at the muddy ground. Jed saw that Jake was leaving
two men with them and rode on ahead of the rest to the grove.
Even here the ground was muck. Jed ground-reined his horse
and spread his slicker. The men dropped among the trees. Jed
was rolling a cigarette when Roy, Ron and Rod rode up. They
sat their horses looking down at him.

"We're going back to headquarters," Roy said flatly. He was
soaking wet and his face was sullen.

"The men can handle the rest," Ron said sourly. "That's
what they're paid to do."

"We done our part and more," Rod added. "No call for you
to treat us like common hands, us your sons."

Jed roared in blind fury and stood rocking on his heels.
When he could talk, he shouted at his three big sons, "You
will stay here where you belong and you will do your share if I
have to rope-whip you."

Two men sitting nearby came over to stand beside Jed. Others shifted on their slickers.

Jed faced Roy. "Climb down," he ordered.

Roy glowered and didn't move.

"Get down," Jed repeated. His anger had turned to a consuming heat but now it was quiet and deadly.

Roy slowly came out of his saddle. He looked defiantly at his father.

"Bring me the bottle," Jed said.

Roy glared for a moment and then unstrapped the saddlebag and took out a half-emptied quart bottle.

"Smash it against a tree," Jed said.

Roy held the bottle by the neck and stared at Jed. He looked undecided and Jed braced himself against the blow to his head that might be coming. He met Roy's burning eyes stonily. At last Roy swung about, walked to a tree and shattered the bottle against the trunk. The sour smell of the whiskey drenched the air.

"Now come here," Jed told him.

When Roy stood before his father, Jed crashed his fist against Roy's jaw. Roy looked stunned and stepped back. He did not lift his arms.

Jed turned to Ron and Rod. "The three of you," he said with a contemptuous glance at Roy. "Ride down to the herd. Send back the two men Jake left. You stay with the cows."

There was hate in each of their eyes, but without another word they rode off to do as they'd been told.

Jed sank to his slicker and leaned against the trunk of a tree. He felt drained. The two men who'd sided him returned to their places. Jed pulled out a bag of Bull Durham and rolled a cigarette. His hands were shaking. He felt someone watching him and looked up. Jake was walking by leading his horse. The range boss was grinning.

The storm fizzled out and Jed dozed. It was midmorning and the sun was breaking through the overcast when Jed awakened. The ground was steaming. He stretched and leaned stiffly away from the tree. The cottonwood was old and damp. There was no sap left in either of them, he thought and faltered to his feet. He looked down to the herd and saw Roy, Rod and Ron sitting together at the near side of the cattle. Damn it, he muttered, you don't sit herd, you ride it. He started to swing into his saddle to ride down and have another go-around with them when the team with the wagon strained up the hill and started around the cows. The men about Jed who were awake left the damp ground and their slickers to stand and watch. At the herd, the three boys started to mount their horses, looking toward the wagon, but Big Jake rode out to meet it and the boys stayed with the bedraggled cows. Jake rode alongside the wagon talking with the driver.

The lumbering, loaded wagon pulled up below Jed and all the hands surrounded it, craning to look into the box. Jake said something to them and they started unloading firewood. Jake rode on up to Jed.

"I sent Little Red," Jake told Jed when he climbed down. He showed some worry lines on his forehead when he thumbed back his hat. "Red says the doc's rig is in the barn."

Jed was relieved. "Decent of the doc to drive out and check on the patient," he observed. "Takes some of the load off Nan's shoulders."

Little Red walked over. He was a small ragtail who wasn't worth his beans but he took orders from Big Jake and followed them without question.

Jake shook his head and asked Jed, "You don't think it's anything else, the doc being there?"

"What else could it be?" Jed demanded. "That gunslinger was near to death. Doc's doing his duty, that's all." He turned to Little Red. "You see or hear anything to make you think otherwise?"

"No," Little Red said after he'd had a minute to think. "I was at the cook shack mostly. Me and Li Shu don't savvy too good and I was told to stay away from the house. The squaws was there, in the house. I saw one of them out for a load of wood."

"There, you see?" Jed told Jake. "Everything is fine. The

squaws were there cooking dinner." He turned back to Little
Red. "What hot grub did Li Shu send?"

Little Red grinned and rubbed his belly. "He'd made a son-
of-a-bitch stew. I brung it and the Arbuckle's and the other
things Jake said."

"Get things moving, Jake," Jed said abruptly. "There's no
time to stand around gabbing. Get the men and horses fed so
we can move out. Little Red can stay here, unload the wagon
and set up camp proper."

During the hot and humid afternoon, the crew worked the
riverbank and draws along the way. The gullies were muddy
ponds that were draining off into the swollen river. They
sluiced cows and calves from the mud and some sheep that had
washed in. The live animals they pushed and roped out. The
dead ones they left to be disposed of later. It was back-breaking
work and Jed grew tighter at each carcass, but it was the sheep
that boiled his gore. They shouldn't have been there with the
cattle. It meant they were grazing on his range or too damned
near. Two ewes were still alive. Jed sent a man back to camp
with them with orders for Little Red to kill and gut them and
string them up. It wasn't much but it made him feel a little
better.

They rounded up a hundred and fifty head that afternoon
but they also found a hundred carcasses. Relieved as Jed was at
each cow that was still standing, he knew his loss was serious
because in addition to the dead cattle in the draws, many
others must have been swept downstream. Another thing began
to gnaw at him. His first acceptance of the doc's appearance at
the ranch that morning was turning to doubt. He thought he
knew why it had worried Jake. It did not seem reasonable the
doc would drive over the treacherous roads in the storm to the
ranch unless something serious had happened to Nan. But
who, he argued with himself, could have gone to town to sum-
mon him? Certainly neither of the squaws nor Li Shu. So it
must have been the doc's concern for his patient who, Jed admitted, was critically wounded.

Despite all he did to reassure himself, anxiety nagged him all afternoon, and when they drove a bunch of muddied cows to the holding area late in the day, he rode back to Jake. "I'm going back to headquarters for an hour or so," he growled. "Maybe bring Li Shu back to do the cooking. I'll take the wagon."

There was a question in Jake's eyes. "I'll go with you," he said.

"You're needed here," Jed said. "You've an hour or so until sundown. Keep the men working. Relieve the boys at supper but see they don't leave camp."

Jake grubbed his beard. "Whyn't you stay at the house tonight?" he suggested. "Get some solid food and some decent sleep in a bed."

Jed felt the oldness in his bones all day but he didn't like Jake seeing it. "If the men can take it, so can I," he snapped. "I'll be back with Li Shu and more grub."

He hadn't fooled Jake, he thought as he slapped the reins on the rumps of the team and rattled the empty wagon down the slope. He was certain Jake knew only worry over Nan could drive him from this roundup.

Doc's rig was still in the barn. Jed left the wagon with the team still hitched and ran to the back door of the house.

"Where's the doc?" he called as Running Doe turned from the range where she was stirring a kettle of broth.

"Upstairs," she said quietly.

It told him all he needed and didn't want to know. It was Nan. Something had happened to Nan. Something very serious to bring the doc out and keep him all day. He hurried up the steps and quietly opened the door to her room. She was in her bed piled with blankets. Doc sat snoozing in a chair beside. His head snapped up at the creak of the hinges. He glanced quickly at Nan and motioned Jed outside.

"What's the matter, what happened?" Jed whispered urgently when they were in the hall.

"She's sleeping now," the doctor said. "Let's go downstairs. You look like you could use a cup of coffee and so could I."

Jed was filled with fear but he waited until they were in the kitchen before he demanded, "Damn it, what's wrong with Nan?"

The doc took a chair at the table and motioned Jed down. His eyes were tired when he peered over his glasses. "She's got the fever," he said.

"The fever!" Jed exclaimed. The word chilled him and angered him. "She caught it from him," he accused, pushing back his chair and half standing, facing the door to the lean-to.

"No," the doc said. His voice was as weary as his eyes. "Sit down, Jed. Running Doe, bring us some coffee. And the brandy. Jed, it's the lung fever. Pneumonia. It's probably been coming on for four or five days. She been acting tired and all worn out lately?"

"Yes," Jed said slowly, remembering, blaming himself for adding the burden of caring for the stranger. He slumped at the table. "She's been plumb tuckered. How bad is she?"

The doc nodded his head. "It was the ride to town in the storm that brought it on, that and the fall she took in the puddle when she sprained her ankle. But it had been coming, it would have brought her down anyway."

"Why'd she ride into town?" Jed exploded.

"To get me, for him." The doc waved his hand toward the lean-to. "He would have died if she hadn't come."

"I wish he had," Jed said bitterly. "Is Nan going to be all right?"

"He didn't send her," the doc said and took the cup of coffee Running Doe brought. He poured brandy in Jed's cup and his. "He's got a fever, too. It's not the same as Nan's. She was worried and came for me because there was no one else to send. It's hard to answer you, Jed. She probably will be all right if the fever breaks."

Jed felt a tightness in his chest and his heart hurt. "When will you know?"

"Tomorrow or the next day." The doc gulped half the coffee and brandy in his cup. "Twenty-four to forty-eight hours, the fever breaks if it's going to."

"If it's going to?" Jed's hand trembled when he lifted his cup.

"I'm doing all I can, everything I know," Doc said. "I wish it was more. I spoon some Dover's to her now and then to keep her sleeping, keep her warm, give her laudanum. Main thing is, keep her warm and hope the fever breaks."

"God," Jed said softly. "You been here all day, Doc, with them. You must be wore out. Get some rest. Tell me what to do, I'll sit up with Nan."

The doc shook his head. "No, Jed. It's mighty contagious. Condition you're in, you'd likely catch it. Can't afford to let you take the risk."

"She's my daughter," Jed said. "Least I can do is be with her when she needs me."

"You come down with it, you're done," Doc said firmly. "Who'd run the ranch, the boys?"

Jed sadly shook his head. "All right, Doc. But I'll be here. Any change, you let me know."

"Sure, Jed. One way or the other."

Suddenly it seemed to Jed that everything had gone wrong since Jake had brought the stranger to the ranch. Anger brought bile to his craw until it almost choked him. He shook his fist at the lean-to door. "He brought all this on. Anything happens to Nan . . ." He stopped and asked more calmly, "How is he?"

"About the same as Nan," Doc said and finished his coffee. "Full Moon is with him, been there all day. If his fever breaks he's got a chance. It's nip and tuck for both of them."

"Is his contagious?" Jed asked.

The doc shook his head.

"Then I'll spell Full Moon," Jed said and pushed back his chair. "She must be tuckered, too. It will give me something to do while I wait."

⦿⦿⦿⦿⦿⦿⦿⦿⦿⦿⦿⦿⦿

# CHAPTER VI

⦿⦿⦿⦿⦿⦿⦿⦿⦿⦿⦿⦿⦿⦿

Nan's fever broke about noon the next day. She felt dizzy and weak when she opened her eyes and gradually became aware that she was in her bed with a mound of blankets over her. She recognized Dr. Bainbridge, who was bending over her feeling her forehead and then taking her pulse.

"What's wrong?" she asked faintly. Even the whisper was an effort.

The doctor smiled. "It's all right now, Nan. Everything is going to be all right. You've been sick with a fever but it's broken. You'll be weak for a while but you'll be all right. The fever is gone."

She remembered now, the ride into town in the storm, the tumble in the puddle, how tired and cold she'd been. "The stranger," she said. "Is he all right?"

The doctor smiled again. "Don't talk anymore. He's going to recover, thanks to you. His fever broke this morning. We'll just have to get some strength in both of you. Your Pa is here. I'll get him if you'll promise not to talk."

"I promise," she whispered.

There was the glint of a tear in Jed's weather-washed eyes when he bent over the bed and kissed Nan's cheek. "You gave us a fright," he said, sitting by the side of the bed and taking her hand.

Nan turned her head to him. He looked as if he hadn't slept for a week. "I'm glad you're here," she said softly.

Jed held up a callused palm. "You're not to talk. Doc's orders. I think I know what's on your mind and I'll try to tell you what I think you want to know. First off, I think it was a brave thing you did, riding in for the doc in the storm. But you shouldn't have done it. No stranger's life is worth a mite of the ill that's come to you." He scowled and chewed his lower lip. "You're wondering how he is. Doc says you saved his life. He's coming out of it but not yet so as he can talk. We don't know who he is or where he come from. Just some saddle tramp. Full Moon is tending him. Running Doe will care for you. Doc has been here better part of two days. He's going back to town after he's been in to see you. I got to get back to the cattle camp. Rode out there early this morning. The men have rounded up something like three hundred head. We'll be moving up to the north range. Hopeful we'll find another three, four hundred. We'll be gone four or five days at least. Your brothers send their love. They're no-count but they think highly of you and being on this drive keeps them out of town. Big Jake sends his regards. I was going to take Li Shu out with me but I'm going to leave him here to cook for you and the stranger and the squaws because they'll both be busy."

He paused and Nan started, "When . . ."

Jed shook his head vigorously. "None of that. Doc'll tell you. You're to stay in bed and eat what Running Doe brings you and not to fret. You listen to the doc and do like he says. I'm going to send Little Red back here. He's not to come into the house but he'll be here and Li Shu can send him to the camp or into town if the doc or anything is needing." He stood, holding Nan's hand in one of his and patting it with the other. "Remember, you mind the doc." At the door he turned and said, "Don't worry about anything. The storm is over and now there will be graze aplenty for what's left of the herd."

Nan nodded her head. Even this small motion took away her breath. "Thank you, Pa," she said.

Doc Bainbridge came in soon after Jed left. A stubble of gray whiskers sprouted from his chin and cheeks, his eyes were filmed with weariness and his clothes were wrinkled but he sat beside her and smiled. "That was a squeaker, Nan," he told her. "You'll not be feeling like riding for a spell and you're to stay in bed until I tell you different. I took the bandage off your ankle. Lucky it was only a sprain. I'll bandage it again and bring you a cane when I come to see you tomorrow so you can hobble around the house when I tell you that you can get up for an hour or two. I'll do that soon as possible. Too much bed rest is bad as not enough. Loses your strength. I'm going to give you another dose of Dover's now. Will help you sleep." He held a glass to her lips and she sipped the bitter-tasting solution. "Running Doe will give you another dose when you've awakened and had some broth."

The doctor stood beside her bed a moment and she asked, "Will the . . . ?"

"I think he'll pull through, Nan. He's not fully regained his senses but I don't think there's any permanent damage and he's a tough young man." He chuckled. "Only thing, he's permanently bald. Hair will never grow back where the Indians scalped him. He'll have to grow it long in front and comb it back. Rest easy, Nan."

"I will, Doctor," she promised.

Running Doe came into the room when the doctor opened the door. She had some towels and a bowl of lime and sulphur in warm water.

"She'll bathe you and give you a fresh nightgown," Doc said. "You'll rest more comfortable."

Nan's thoughts were on the stranger while she felt the soothing warm towels gently massage her skin. Pa had said he was a saddle tramp but she wondered. She wondered what had happened to him and, too, who Emma was. Perhaps it was because she'd tended him and ridden into town for help, she realized, but she felt strangely drawn to the man who lay on the cot in the lean-to.

When Nan awakened, the ceiling swayed dizzily and for a moment she didn't know where she was. It was daytime because sunlight flowed in a bright golden stream through the west window, which she faced. Gradually she remembered that she had been ill. She felt very tired. In a hypersensitive condition, she sensed that something was wrong. She turned her head and saw Running Doe standing, defiant and angry, at the door. She lifted her head a little and saw Big Jake, huge and black-bearded, filling the doorway.

Enfeebled as she was, Nan was outraged. Except when Jed called Big Jake to his office, he never entered the white house. Shakily, she propped herself on her elbow. "What are you doing here?" she gasped.

Big Jake twisted his hat by the brim in both hands and shuffled his boots. Above his beard, his cheekbones colored. "Meaning no disrespect," he muttered. "I rode in with Little Red to pick up a bag of beans. Thought you'd be sleeping and just come up quiet to ask Running Doe how you was."

Nan began to shake. "This is outrageous," she said. "Get out of my bedroom."

Jake repeated, "Meaning no disrespect."

Nan felt her limbs begin to tremble. "Go," she ordered.

Jake's voice was surly when he said, "Didn't mean to upset you but didn't think it out of place for a old friend to look in, specially seeing how you was alone in the house with him down there. Was worried about that."

Nan collapsed and her head fell back on the pillow. She felt Running Doe step toward the hall. "It's no concern of yours," Nan whispered.

"Oh, yes it is," Jake said. "It's all our concern. If harm was to come to you . . ."

Uncontrollable sobs shook Nan.

"You go," Running Doe told Jake.

"Keep out of this," Jake snarled. His voice was not mean but stern when he told Nan, "You're not to see him down there when you're up and around. You're not to go near the lean-to. You understand?"

She could not answer but she heard his boots clattering down the steps.

Dr. Bainbridge was astonished the next day at the relapse Nan seemed to have suffered.

⊚⊚⊚⊚⊚⊚⊚⊚⊚⊚⊚⊚⊚⊚

# CHAPTER VII

⊚⊚⊚⊚⊚⊚⊚⊚⊚⊚⊚⊚⊚⊚

For fitful and brief periods during the next days, Handy Southern was aware that he was helpless in strange surroundings but sensed he was being cared for in a friendly atmosphere. Sometimes, when he was conscious, someone would lift spoons of water or broth to his lips. Seemingly unrelated events flashed across his mind in nightmarish lack of sequence and he could not relate to them. A savage image of some long-fanged animal would stab pain into his chest. Indians brutalized victims on a limitless desert. His throat parched although a spoon of water was in his mouth. One time when he opened his eyes, he looked into the dark, stolid face of an Indian and he cringed with fear although it was only the face of a squaw.

Then one morning he awakened perfectly lucid with clear recollection of all that had happened up to the time he'd crawled into Green River. From there on his mind was blank. Someone, he told himself, had found him helpless and nursed him back to life.

"Where am I?" he asked the squaw who sat beside his bed. He did not think it strange that an Indian woman should be tending him.

"You wait, I tell her," the squaw said and shush-shushed from the room.

From the cooking smells that seeped under the door, he knew he was in a small room off a kitchen. There was movement in the kitchen and occasionally he heard the scrape of metal, perhaps a spoon stirring in a pot or kettle. He could smell coffee and suddenly he wanted a cup of coffee more than he'd ever craved a shot of whiskey. He remembered his wounds and touched them. His bandaged side was stiff, his buttocks tender. He hesitated to touch his skull. When he did he found it salved, loosely covered and numb. His kneecaps were scabbed, as were his hands.

Someone had brought him here, treated his wounds and cared for him. He felt such a deep sense of gratitude that his breath hurt in his chest. He tried to push himself up to look around but his arms would not support him. All he could see was the chair where the squaw had sat and the whitewashed board wall beyond.

He heard the door open and the uneven, limping walk of feminine steps approached his cot. When he twisted his head and looked, he saw a young lady he had never seen before, not even in his dreams. She seemed pale and fragile but this only enhanced the uncommon beauty of her. An aura seemed to shimmer from the golden bounty of her hair. She wore a man's shirt, open at the throat, and Levis.

"Welcome back to our world," she said and smiled. Her voice was low and musical although a little faint.

"Before I ask anything," he said when she sat beside him, "thank you. They are poor words to tell what I feel. I know you nursed me back to life."

"Not me," she said. "I left my own sickbed only yesterday."

"Where am I?"

"At the Lazy J ranch, north from Green River. Do you remember Green River?"

"I was trying to get there. I don't remember that I did. What happened?"

"You crawled into town and collapsed." She bent over, lifted his head and adjusted his pillow so he was propped a little. "Is that better?"

"Yes." He could see her better.

"Our foreman found you on the street," she said, sitting back. "He carried you to the doctor and, when your wounds were bandaged, brought you here. Is all this talk tiring you?"

"No. I want to talk. What is his name? I can never repay

him." He thought she frowned slightly. "How long have I been here?"

"Jake. They call him Big Jake. He and the others are all out on the range. Today is the sixth day since he brought you."

He was astonished. Six days of his life he'd never know. "It was kind of you to care for me. You don't know me."

She smiled. "I told you, it was not me but the Indian woman Full Moon who has been with you day and night. I am Nan. Who are you?"

"Handy Southern," he said and coughed. It hurt his side and he winced.

"I've stayed too long," she said in immediate concern. "Sleep now."

"No," he said earnestly. "Don't go. I've been by myself a long time." He thought a shadow briefly clouded her eyes. "I'm all right. Only a little weak. I felt faint just then."

"I'll get you some broth," she said at once and laughed lightly when she stood. "That's what they fed me while I was in bed. I never want to taste broth again. Would you like a soft-boiled egg? I think that would be all right."

He grinned although it stretched the skin tightly over his cheekbones. "What I'd really like is a cup of coffee. Although I don't know how I'd manage. My arms won't support me."

"Let me worry about that," she said, briskly for someone who'd been sick herself. She walked from the room favoring her right foot.

He was tired but he willed himself to stay awake and alert. He had never experienced a time such as this and did not want it to pass.

She brought a cup of black coffee and, although he preferred it with canned milk and sugar, he did not complain. She sat on the chair beside the cot and fed it to him from a spoon. It was hot and strong and tasted very good to him.

"Where are you from?" she asked.

"I rode here from Cheyenne," he said.

"Do you remember what happened to you? Don't answer if it will pain you."

"I don't want to forget," he said grimly. "Indians jumped me, shot my horse and me, scalped me. A wolf bit me. When I couldn't walk, I started to crawl." He was suddenly aware of his dependence and poverty. He didn't even have a horse. "I heard they were hiring in Green River, but from what I saw it's as burnt up here as in the East."

"There was a storm the night you came," she said and gave him another spoon of coffee. "Lucky you did crawl or you'd have surely drowned even on the trail. We lost several hundred head. Pa and my brothers and Jake and all the rest except one have been out almost a week rounding up everything that's still on four legs. But now the grass is showing green."

"Run many head?"

"About a thousand. More like six or seven hundred now."

Handy's hope of finding work here on the Lazy J where he could see and sometimes talk with Nan faded. There wouldn't be enough to do for the hands they had. If they could find anything for him, he'd work for board and bunk just to be near her. "I'm sorry," he said. "About the herd."

"Worse has happened and Pa's pulled out of it, always better than before." Her eyes suddenly were amused and she smiled slightly. "If it's work that's troubling you, don't let it. I know Jake. He wouldn't have bothered with you if he didn't have something in mind."

"He doesn't know me, doesn't know what I can do," Handy said. "But whatever it may be, I'll do it gladly. I've never owed a man so much. Him for carrying me to the doctor and bringing me here. And you and your father for taking me in."

She smiled. "We can commiserate while we recuperate." Then she laughed softly. "I never would have used those words with any of the men. Not that I talk down to them. But the way you speak, well, it isn't the same."

"I know," he said ruefully. "I've had to fight my way out from many a corner because of it. My father was a schoolteacher in Ohio before he came West to take up ranching. He taught Sis and me." He thought Nan's eyes were troubled again and he added, "You said you were just up from your sickbed. What was it ailed you?"

"The doctor says I had pneumonia or lung fever as some call it. High fever and aching bones and coughing. I'm still a little shaky. As for the foot, I let my pony stumble and sprained my ankle."

"I've dirtied my shirt more than once," he said and grinned. Again he felt the skin stretch stiffly over bone.

She sat quietly for a moment without speaking, then, unexpectedly, she asked softly, "Who is Emma?"

He was startled. "How did you know?" He considered. "I must have talked in my delirium. Emma was my sister."

"Your sister?" He thought he detected a note of relief in her voice.

"Yes. We had a small spread near Fort Benton in Montana Territory. Pa left it to the two of us. The Sioux from Dakota Territory raided us. Emma was killed and the ranch burned out. I was at Fort Benton and that's what I found when I returned. Emma's body and the embers of the house and barn. They'd driven off the horses and the cattle. I went a little crazy and took the trail after them. I never did catch up with them. I couldn't go back, not after what had happened, so I've been drifting, working when I could."

"Oh!" Nan's breath caught. "I'm so sorry."

"So am I, but it's the chance you take in the West. The Indians killed my father, too. You must have your own problems here."

"Yes, but not the tragic things that have happened to you. Your father, sister, you, almost. You must really hate the Indians."

"I do," he said flatly. "Even the old squaw who's been sitting here with me all the time. I should be grateful to her but I can't be."

"You shouldn't blame them all for what has been done by a few, but I understand," Nan said. "From now on, I'll take her place."

Handy's heart beat a little faster at thought of Nan sitting and talking with him each day but he said, "It is very kind but beyond all reason. The squaw has been good to me. I need to learn to bury my feelings."

Nan laughed. "Nonsense. It will give me something to do while I'm housebound and help me to regain my strength."

"I would like that," he said frankly.

Nan was silent for a moment, then she said, "The drouth has been our big problem. Another problem is the sheepmen. They've been moving onto the open range. This always has been cattle country—the sheep spoil the graze. This year, with the drouth, it's been worse than ever. There's bad feeling. The sheep are an obsession with my father. I fear what may come of it."

The door swung open and Handy screwed his head around to find a small old man, dark and wrinkled as a burned boot, standing in the doorway.

"Pa!" Nan exclaimed and limped to him. She put her arms around him and he kissed her cheek, eyes looking over her shoulder to examine Handy.

"Glad to see the cripples are mending," he observed dryly to Nan. "Doc say you could be up and around?"

"Oh, yes," she said and stepped aside. "Yesterday. He said he wanted me up for several hours every day, that it would help me regain my strength." She turned to Handy. "This is my Pa, Jed. Pa, this is Handy Southern. He only today fully regained his senses."

"I'm grateful to you, sir," Handy said, "to all of you for the attention you've given me. For taking me in when I was near dead and giving me life again."

A large, dark-bearded form loomed behind Jed and Nan.

"And, Handy, this is Jake, our foreman, who carried you to the doctor and brought you here," Nan said. A curious frown puckered her forehead.

Handy thought the big man's eyes looked like turquoise stones. They were flat and there was nothing in them. Without speaking, Jake turned and stomped across the kitchen floor before Handy could thank him for all he'd done.

# CHAPTER VIII

Despite the discomfort from his wounds and his awkward position on his stomach, the next few weeks were the brightest Handy had ever experienced. Each morning after Full Moon had bathed and shaved him and changed the bandages, Nan brought his breakfast on a tray. For the first days, it was soft, a boiled egg or mush which she fed him. As his strength returned there were pancakes, steaks and potatoes and she placed the tray on the chair so he could feed himself. She seemed to realize that to restore confidence in himself, he needed to be free of dependence on the women.

After she'd taken the tray back to the kitchen, she'd return with two cups of coffee and sit and talk with him by the hour. She'd regained her health and her limp was gone. She spent most afternoons in the saddle and her face was richly tanned. In the shirt and Levis she always wore, she looked robust and spirited. She usually sounded breathless, as if she had been running, and made the daily routine at the ranch sound exciting.

"Juliet foaled today, that's my pony's mother," she exuberated one morning. "A spanking youngster even on his wobbly legs." And, eyes jubilant: "Pa says the new grass is putting some beef on the cattle, that we'll come out even though we lost almost three hundred head." And: "The fishing hole's come back. I caught a three-pound cutthroat this afternoon. We'll have the trout for breakfast."

She was lively and lovely and Handy looked forward to his mornings with her.

Full Moon brought the dinner tray at noon after which

Handy would sleep. Jed usually brought the supper tray and would stay to talk while Handy ate. He liked to talk about his younger years when he'd been building up the ranch.

"I got deed land now, about a thousand acres. Mostly we run the herd on the north range, that and open range, in summer. When I come here from Texas it all was open range and you used what you could take and hold on to. There was Indians and rustlers and land grabbers and you had to be handy with a gun." He looked sharply at Handy for a moment. "I was damned handy. Notched my share of scallops. You ever been in a shoot-out?"

"Yes," Handy admitted slowly. There had been that time at Fort Benton, he'd won a hundred dollars in a pot and the heavy loser had accused him of cheating. Handy picked up his winnings and walked out rather than get into a barroom brawl. They knew him in Fort Benton, respected his fists and feared his temper, but the tinhorn who'd lost the $100 was a newcomer. He followed Handy into the street and drew as he called him down. The newcomer drew first but Handy fired first and dropped the man.

When Handy didn't elaborate, he thought he read approval in Jed's eyes. "What gun you favor?" Jed asked.

"Single-action Walker Colt .44," he answered promptly. "I like its heft."

Jed chuckled. "Nine pounds is a lot of heft. What's your choice in rifles?"

"Henry .44 repeating rifle," Handy answered. "Maybe a little old-fashioned like the Walker Colt but I like the way it reaches out and slams them down. And I like the cartridges being interchangeable with the Colt."

"I split a cartwheel, side edge on, with a Henry," Jed said, "at fifty yards."

"Don't know I could match that," Handy said and laughed, "but I did put three slugs on a cartwheel in the air before it fell, with the Colt."

When he thought about it later, Handy realized that most of

his conversations with Jed had been about guns, but that seemed understandable.

"They're my weakness, guns are," Jed had said. "Got a cabinet full of them, Walker Colt and Henry included. When you're about, I'll let you use them now and then to keep your hand and eye in shape."

"I'd be proud," Handy had said. "Haven't had a Henry against my shoulder for a time. Last rifle was a Winchester until the Indians lifted that and my hair. I'd like to get against a Henry once more." He was vastly impressed with the thoughtfulness of Nan and Jed and wondered at the interest they were showing in him. He also wondered at Big Jake, the man who'd really saved his life. He never did come by to have a cup of coffee or talk.

About the only annoyance Handy felt was when one or another of Jed's sons slipped into the lean-to, always when Jed was away from the house and Nan was out on her pony. He wondered whether the three brothers ever did any work. Their time seemed to be their own.

"Enjoy yourself while you can," Roy badgered. He always seemed to be sneering. "You're running up quite a account."

"I realize that," Handy said evenly. "I'm anxious to be up and start to work it off."

"I think not," Roy said flatly. "You got Nan coming in to see you and the squaws to wait on you and a bed with sheets in the white house. Never heard tell of a saddle tramp having life so good."

Or Rod would slam in, face flushed with whiskey, and bellow, "How long you going to lay there like you was sick? You got Nan and Pa buffaloed but not us. When you going to get out to the bunkhouse where you belong? You're near filled out and big as me. Jake's got work for you to do."

And Ron, arms dangling over his big belly, would come to the door and stand looking disgustedly at Handy without speaking. Then he'd snort and walk away.

Pleasant as were the mornings with Nan and the evenings with Jed, Handy was beginning to chafe at his helpless, bedridden state. He waited to be up and about, to start paying off the debt he was accumulating. He felt his strength was returning. He could push himself from the cot and get up on his knees, which he did for exercise. The wound in his side was healed and the bandage removed. His head would never be the same and he'd have to keep his skull covered outdoors but it, too, was healed. He felt almost back to normal. Only the mutilated buttock kept him off his feet.

"Wolf bite can't be all that bad," he told Doc Bainbridge the next time he came by. "Man can't spend his whole life in bed on his belly."

The doc laughed and over his glasses his eyes twinkled. "I know it must be wearisome but that wolf took a big chunk of your flesh, what little there was of it, right down to the bone. We had to give your body a chance to rebuild some protective tissue. You'll always have a hole there where part of your butt used to be but at least it will be covered. Let's see how it looks today."

He pulled off the bandage and probed at the healing wound. Handy could feel the tight tissue under the doctor's finger. "It's going to be tender for a while when you sit," the doc said. "Use a pillow. You won't be in a saddle for a time but there's no reason why you can't get up, move around, walk a bit. Exercise in moderation will do you good. You can sleep on your side. We'll keep it salved and bandaged a bit longer. Don't overdo. I'll speak to Jed." He studied Handy a long moment. At last he said, "You got guts, young man. Night Jake lugged you into my office I had my doubts and I never thought you'd make it when you came down with the fever and Nan rode in for me in that fierce storm."

Handy tucked the pillow under him and sat on the edge of the cot. The unaccustomed movement made him dizzy for a minute. When his head stopped swimming, he said in slow, demanding words, "Nan did what?"

The doc looked surprised. "Didn't you know? You came on with a high bad fever. Nan was sitting with you and it frightened her. There was no one here. All the men were out trying to drive the cattle to high ground. She saddled up her pony and rode through that storm over the road that wasn't fit to travel to Green River. Her pony stumbled and fell and that's how she came to sprain her ankle. That ride brought on pneumonia. Didn't cause it, she had that in her, but it brought it on. Nan saved your life that morning."

The gratitude Handy felt to Nan was large and warm.

The doc must have talked with Jed because shortly after Handy heard the doc's buggy leave, Jed came in with a bundle of clothes. "Doc says you can be about a bit," he said and smiled. "Glad to hear it. Anxious to see what you can really do with them guns. Here's some of Rod's things left from when he was still living in the house. You're about the same size now but you'll best him by fifty pounds one day unless you keep lean and trim. Take things easy. Don't want a relapse."

Handy thought it passing strange, the way Jed always went back to guns.

The plaid shirt was a little garish for Handy's taste and a little tight across the shoulders but the Levis were right in the waist and length and the boots the proper size and not worn much. When he stood, his legs were weak under his weight and he swayed when he tottered into the kitchen, skull protected by a pad and covered with the flat-crowned black hat Jed had given him.

Full Moon turned from the range when he walked into the kitchen and smiled at him. It was a friendly, genuine smile and so unexpected that he impulsively went to her and patted her meaty shoulder. "Thank you," he told her. "You took care of me and helped me get well."

Immediately her face turned to a sculpted chunk of brown granite and she was her stolid self again, as if the show of emotion had been a weakness on the part of each of them.

When he'd had a cup of coffee, he stepped off the stoop into the backyard, filling his lungs with great gulps of the sweet, clean afternoon air. It was as if he could not breathe in enough. The sun was warm and bright and glinted on the rippling river beyond the cottonwood trees. The stream had receded in the weeks following the storm but still was running a good flow. He looked to the hills beyond the lodge-pole corral and horse pasture and it pleased him to find them tinted green. It was a good day to be at the Lazy J and alive and mending.

He started toward the long, low bunkhouse, painted white like the house and barn and cook shack. He had little hope of finding Jake there at this afternoon hour but thought he'd try. He wanted to acknowledge his enormous debt to the range boss as soon as possible and tell him he'd be ready to go to work as soon as the doc said he could. He also wanted to let Jake know that he was capable of earning his keep at whatever job Jake had in mind.

"Handy!" It was a delighted cry and it came from the barn.

He turned carefully and found Nan running toward him. He grinned and lifted a hand in greeting.

"When? How?" she asked breathlessly. Her hat was hanging by the thong on the back of her neck. Her golden hair was tousled and small beads of perspiration jeweled her forehead.

"Doc Bainbridge said some small exercise wouldn't hurt." He laughed. "I've got to sit on a pillow for a while."

She took his arm. "If we can't ride together for a while, we'll walk together," she said lightly. "Your head?"

"Got to keep it covered. Doc says the hair won't grow back."

"Lots of men are bald," she dismissed his hair. "Anyway, you can get a wig to wear when you go to town."

He stopped, looking at her and chuckling. "I hadn't thought of a hairpiece. That would be the answer."

They wandered toward the river, he moving cautiously on his unsure legs, she holding his arm and sometimes catching him when he seemed to hesitate. Nan was Jed's daughter and Handy was worse than a penniless hand. He knew it was out of the question, but after the weeks they'd spent together his heart went out to her.

"Nan," he said quietly, "I didn't know until today that you'd ridden through that storm for the doctor and that it had brought on your pneumonia. Someday I hope I can show you how much everything you have done for me means to me."

"Nonsense," she said, but she looked serious and they walked in silence. He felt very close to her.

At his gait, it took them more than an hour to walk to the river and back. The hands were riding in from the range as they neared the house. They all turned to stare at Nan and Handy, especially the hulking black-bearded man who hazed a buckskin toward the corral.

"That's Big Jake, isn't it?" he asked Nan. "I've got to talk to him, thank him proper."

She let him go without a word.

Jake had hung his saddle on the fence and was coming toward Handy, heading for the bunkhouse.

"Oh, Jake," Handy called while the range boss was still a dozen paces off.

Jake's curiously stony, turquoise eyes observed Handy as he strode past without a word. Handy thought he had never seen such a look of sheer hatred.

◎◎◎◎◎◎◎◎◎◎◎◎◎

# CHAPTER IX

◎◎◎◎◎◎◎◎◎◎◎◎◎

It bothered Handy that there should be bad feeling between Big Jake and himself. He thought he knew what had caused it and resolved to do something about it after supper.

Nan had propped a pillow on a chair at the big round table in the kitchen and he had supper with her and Jed. She had changed from shirt and Levis and wore a long white apron over a yellow-checked gingham dress. She looked more feminine than Handy had ever seen her. She did the cooking and the room was fragrant with the good, homey smells of hot biscuits, saddle of venison, baked potatoes and coffee. She'd even baked a cherry pie. There wasn't much conversation but Nan looked flushed and pleased each time he glanced at her. Jed, too, had a satisfied look on his leathery face.

"How'd it go today?" he asked when they'd reached their second cups of coffee.

"Getting off that cot was the best thing that's happened to me," Handy said heartily. "I've been feeling better by the hour. There should be something I can do to earn my keep until I'm able to climb back into the saddle."

Jed nodded his head soberly. "There will be, when the time comes, but we're not going to rush things. I had a talk with the doc and he said how it had to be. For now take things easy like you did today."

Handy didn't want to but he felt he had to say it. "I think I'd better move into the bunkhouse tomorrow."

Nan cried, "No." It must have slipped out because she looked embarrassed.

Jed looked surprised. "Why?"

"The men," Handy said, "if I'm ever going to get along with them. Long as I was bedridden, I suppose they could tolerate the idea of my being here in your house. Now they've seen me walking around, they'll expect me to bunk with them where I belong. You've treated me like a special guest. The men resent it, even Big Jake who brought me here. I wanted to talk with him this afternoon but he'd have none of it. Walked past like I wasn't there."

"I'll have a talk with Jake," Jed said angrily. "He can tell the men. There's reasons you stay right here awhile longer, until you're stronger and the doc says it's safe for you to move. You're still shaky. You got to sit on a pillow. How would that look in the cook shack and bunkhouse?" He grinned and his old face cracked into wrinkles. "Got another reason and that's personal. Feel up to a shooting match tomorrow?"

Handy held out his right hand. It was pale but it was steady. "Yep," he said. "But I don't want Jake feeling bad blood toward me. I'd better go to the bunkhouse. I can take care of myself."

"You stay here like I say," Jed said stubbornly.

Nan looked relieved when Handy made no further objections. He'd have enjoyed staying up and talking with Nan and Jed over another cup of coffee but his first day on his feet had tired him. He excused himself and went to his cot. Jed's reasons for paying such particular attention to him continued to puzzle him. The old man certainly knew him for what he was, a hand who was broke and out of work with no especial skills or talents. What could Jed expect of him? He worried the thought until he fell asleep.

After breakfast the next morning, again alone in the kitchen with Nan and Jed, the rancher took Handy into his office. It was a small room with a rolltop desk and safe but there was a large oak cabinet where Jed kept his collection of guns. He had all of them from Colt's first successful model, the "Texas," a single-action .44 without a trigger guard, on through the years. There was the nine-pound, nine-inch-barrel Walker Colt .44 named after the Texas Ranger captain, Samuel Walker, who had suggested it to Colt, and the single-action Army Colt which the manufacturer had brought out in 1870. Jed had heavy buffalo guns and Henry and Winchester repeating rifles. There were odd guns, the "Gambler's" gun, a .41-caliber gun of short range, fitted in a .45 frame, single-action, and a light-weight double-action gun of the same caliber; and there were derringers and pepperboxes.

"Pick out a gun and rifle that suits," Jed said.

Without hesitation, Handy took the Walker Colt and Henry. Jed selected a .45-caliber model of the single-action Army and a Winchester 30-30. When Handy buckled on the gun belt and holstered the gun, he felt fully dressed. Jed must have read the satisfaction Handy felt because he chuckled.

Handy was feeling stronger and much better this morning but he could not keep up with the old man's stride.

"Sorry," Jed said. He slowed to match Handy's gait.

"It's all right," Handy assured him. "I've got to learn to keep up again."

"You will, son, you will, in less time than you think," Jed told him.

Handy shook his head. Jed's attitude confused him. He was sure Jed didn't treat his own sons with the same consideration.

They walked south, away from the house, until they approached a gray old haystack in a field that looked as if it were used as a winter feed lot. Jed had rigged an ingenious device with the haystack behind it. He had mounted a wagon wheel on a cut-down axle. Playing cards, all aces, were nailed to every third spoke. The axle was well greased and the wheel spun rapidly when Jed gave it a turn.

"Get the idea?" he asked.

Handy grinned. "Yep. Beats all I've ever seen."

"Did it myself," Jed said and chuckled. "Thought it up and built it. Proud of it, I am. Takes a man who can shoot to hit them pips." He stepped off twenty-five paces. "First the revolver at fifteen yards," he said.

Handy loaded all six cylinders, laid the barrel across his forearm and fired carefully and deliberately. The gun lifted in re-

coil with each shot and he brought the barrel back to rest each
time before firing again. He plunked six of the aces dead
center.

"That kind of shooting is all right for target practice," Jed
said disapprovingly. "Now five beans in the wheel."

Handy laughed. He was being put to the test. He left the cyl-
inder under the hammer open and holstered the gun. Jed gave
the wheel another turn, stepped aside and called, "Now."

Handy drew, cocking the gun in the web between his thumb
and forefinger. When he fired his first shot, he held the trigger
back. The recoil of the gun cocked it each time and his fire was
rapid. He hit three of the pips flat on and nicked the fourth
and fifth.

Jed drew and pulled off five shots in rapid succession when
Handy spun the wheel. He was dead center with all five.

"Now the rifles," Jed said. He stepped off six hundred paces.
"Six hundred yards, more or less. I'll go back and give the
wheel a twist. Shoot when I call. Do it standing. Anybody can
shoot straight on his belly."

Handy stood sidewise to the whirling target. At Jed's com-
mand he levered off six fast shots. He did not hit any pips but
he was close with each shot.

Handy replaced Jed at the wheel. The old marksman gave
himself a penalty of another hundred yards. When Handy had
the target twirling, Jed knocked off six shots as rapidly as
Handy had fired. He was near dead center with each one.

"I'm afraid I'm not in your class," Handy told Jed as they
sauntered back to the ranch house.

Jed chuckled. "You'll do, you'll do." He turned his sharp
eyes briefly on Handy. There was a pleased expression on his
face. "That was mighty fine shooting, taking in allowance you
was just off your sickbed. Ain't many could match it and the
guns was strange. Come out here in the mornings and practice.
Help pass away the time."

Again, Handy knew he was being accorded privileges not
given other hands, including Big Jake. The feeling returned

that Jed expected something from him. He could not understand what it could be.

When Jed had put the guns in the cabinet, he rode out to the range where some of the men were still searching for strays that had escaped the storm. Handy went to the kitchen for a cup of coffee. He had not seen Nan since breakfast and felt aimless. He wondered what he could do this day.

Nan came down the steps and sat at the table with him. She was wearing a light silk white dress and a round white hat. "What were you and Pa doing out there?" she asked.

Handy laughed. "Target shooting. I guess I bragged some I could shoot and he showed me up." He shook his head in admiration. "I never saw shooting the way he does."

Nan pinched her forehead with a frown that put small lines between her eyes. "It's passing strange," she said. "Pa's not worn a gun nor fired a shot even at a target in more than three years. He was gunned down and nearly died. He swore he'd never wear a gun again. He believes in the code of the West, that no one will fire at an unarmed man." She shrugged and smiled. "He must have taken a fancy to you."

So that meant that Jed had taken the trouble to fix up and grease the target wheel that morning, Handy thought. And taken Handy out to relieve the monotony he thought Handy must be suffering. "I can't believe anyone could outshoot your father," he said.

"He was ambushed," Nan said. "He maintains they were gunmen, hired by the sheepmen."

"If they were," Handy said slowly, "it wouldn't have mattered whether or not he was armed." Handy wondered whether the reason Jed was treating him as he was could be sympathy because Handy, too, had been ambushed. He put away the thought and smiled at her. "I missed our morning talk," he said. "You doing something special today? You look mighty fine in a dress and hat."

"Well, thank you, sir," she said and laughed. "I'm going to town, to the dressmaker. Come with me. I'm taking the buggy." She giggled. "We'll take a pillow for you and you can go see Doc Bainbridge. I think that's a good idea anyway, for him to check you to make sure you're not overdoing right at the start."

"I'd like that," he said frankly, pleased and flattered.

It was an odd but pleasant feeling for a working cowboy to be riding in a buggy with a beautiful young lady holding the reins. He was relieved the men were all on the range and none saw Nan and him drive off. Under the circumstances, he thought, he probably should have stayed on the ranch.

"I do not understand the kindness and thoughtfulness you and your father have shown me," he said as they started down the rutted road to Green River in the bright, warm morning. "It isn't that I'm not grateful. I am, deeply. But Jed doesn't know I'm worth my found. Neither of you know a thing about me."

"I do," she said softly. "We've been together every day for weeks. I know you well, Handy Southern, and I approve of what I've learned. Pa respects courage more than anything in the world. He knows what you went through." She laughed. "Don't worry. He'll find something for you to do that he'll consider repayment."

When they reached Doc Bainbridge's house and he climbed out, she remained uncertainly at the fence and he walked back to the buggy. "Is there something?" he asked.

"Yes," she said. "I mean no offense, Handy, but please take this." She handed him a cartwheel. "Consider it a loan. You can repay me when you're able to work. I'll be by Trail's End saloon for you in about two hours."

"Thank you and no offense," he said with a smile. "But no thank you." He returned the silver dollar. "When I'm through here, I'll look over the town, go into the saloon and watch the game. I'll be out in front in two hours."

The doc was pleased with Handy's condition, especially after he reported his activities. "Another week and I think we can take off the diapers," he said with a twinkle in his eyes. "How you getting along with them out at the Lazy J?"

"The finest, most thoughtful and considerate people I've ever known," Handy said sincerely.

"Yes, well." Doc Bainbridge peered over the tops of his glasses and his eyes were steely. "Big Jake, too?"

"I haven't even talked with him. I've tried to, to thank him for what he did, but he seems to be avoiding me, or resent me. Would there be a reason for him to feel like that?"

"Maybe." The doc did not elaborate but he did comment, "Big Jake's as ornery a critter as ever rode the range. He'd as soon wring your neck as a chicken's." Abruptly he laughed. "You're fleshing out, Handy. You were a skeleton when he brought you in. By the time you fill out your big-boned frame and all your strength is back, I don't think even Big Jake will cross your path. Is it true that faint as you were, you clubbed to death that wolf that tried to make a meal of you?"

"I guess so," Handy said absently. "What's the reason he's got it in for me? Because they been caring for me at the white house?"

"Could be that's part of it," the doc agreed. "Could be he knows he's got a bear by the tail."

"I thought my being at the house might stir up some feelings," Handy said. "I told Jed last night I wanted to move into the bunkhouse but he insisted I stay in the lean-to until you took off the bandages on my rump."

"I'd listen to Jed," the doc cautioned. "How'd you get to town?"

"Nan." Handy laughed. "In a buggy sitting on a pillow."

The doc's eyes were hard as they carefully examined Handy. Finally he said, "You'll do. Another week or two and you'll do."

It was a strange remark for the doc to make. It was not unlike what Jed had said that morning.

Handy had wandered around town, watched a bloody fight between a sheepherder and a cow poke, observed the small and listless poker game at the Trail's End and was leaning against the hitch rail in front of the saloon when Nan drove up.

"You must be tired," she said contritely when he settled on

the pillow and breathed with relief. "I forgot about your sitting problem."

"Doc says he'll turn me loose in another week."

"Oh." Nan bit her lower lip and spanked the team. "I suppose that means you'll move to the bunkhouse."

"And go to work. High time."

"I'll miss you, Handy," she said. She handed him a paper bag. "I thought perhaps you might be missing this."

He opened the sack. In it were twelve bags of Bull Durham and papers. "How did you know?" he asked, pleased. "I haven't really craved them until today, in the saloon." He paused, opened a sack of tobacco and built a smoke. Carefully, he said, "I'll miss you, too, Nan. It won't be the same." He wished he had a spread of his own. He was in love with Nan. The circumstances were hopeless and he knew it. The sooner he moved to the bunkhouse, the better it would be for both of them.

They drove out of town and started for the ranch without speaking further. After a mile, Nan said, "We'll go on a picnic tomorrow. I know a place down the river, the fishing pool. It's usually full even when the river is low. There must be springs. I'll fix a lunch and we'll take the buggy. Or we can fish and catch our lunch."

He started to tell her that regardless of what Jed or the doc said, he was going to move into the bunkhouse that afternoon, but before he could, she giggled and said, "I'll take the pillow for you so you'll be comfortable and not disturb the fish."

She looked so eager at the prospect of the picnic, he didn't have the heart to mention the bunkhouse. Besides, he liked the idea of the picnic himself. Another day shouldn't make too much difference.

They were almost at the turnoff to the ranch when they met Big Jake. Nan slowed the team and lifted her hand in greeting. Handy leaned over to shout halloo.

Jake spurred his horse and galloped by without touching his hat to Nan.

◎◎◎◎◎◎◎◎◎◎◎◎

# CHAPTER X

◎◎◎◎◎◎◎◎◎◎◎◎

From the lean-to window, the early morning sky was lilac blue and salmon pink. There was promise of a fine, fair summer day, an ideal day for a picnic. Handy faced the day with mixed emotions. The prospect of a day on the river with Nan excited and gladdened him yet there would be sadness. He had decided he must tell her this would be their last day together, that he could no longer delay moving to the bunkhouse. Their encounter with Big Jake the day before had convinced him. The ranch foreman's disrespect to Nan was because of him, he knew.

Although Handy was up early, Full Moon told him Jed had already eaten. Nan had not yet come down. He was finishing his eggs, steak and fried potatoes when loud, angry voices from Jed's office drew his attention. Without wanting to eavesdrop, he could not help overhearing the argument. He recognized Jed's voice and the other, he was sure, was Jake's. They were arguing about him.

Jed was shouting, "The doc says he's to stay here and not work until the bandage is off his butt."

"The men don't take kindly to it," Jake roared. "They see him walking around, riding off to town in the buggy, living and eating here in the house. They know he's going to be a hand like them when he's able. They say, why in hell ain't he treated like the rest?"

"I don't have to explain what I do to you or them," Jed yelled, "but you know the answer to that."

"I do, but I can't tell the men," Jake barked. "Far as they're concerned he's just another hand when he can ride. He's got to go to the bunkhouse and eat in the cook shack and stop gallivanting around with Nan. Otherwise they're going to start to drift. You want to keep him here like he's your guest, that's a different story. I'll tell the men that but then he can never throw in with them."

"If I was sure, that's exactly what I'd do," Jed said, quieter. "But I ain't sure. I want him working for me as a hand."

"Then, damnit, he goes to the bunkhouse and gets no more special treatment," Jake snapped. "I'll find work for him to do that won't take no great strength or fester his wound."

"Don't tell me what to do," Jed stormed. "I'm the one that gives the orders."

The exchange was puzzling to Handy but the situation had reached the point he'd feared. He pushed back his chair and went across the living room to Jed's office. Jake's eyes were hard and flat when he turned to the doorway. Jed was at his desk. His piercing eyes narrowed.

"Couldn't help hearing," Handy said. He turned to Jake. "Been meaning to talk to you before but never seemed to catch up with you. Wanted to thank you proper for saving my life, picking me off the street and bringing me out here." He looked at Jed. "It's been in my mind that I ought to move in with the men, like I told you yesterday."

Jed's fist hit the desk. "Damnit, Handy, you only been on your feet two days. The doc was in to talk to me. He told me what you had to do."

"I'll be as well off at the bunkhouse," Handy said quietly. "I can change the bandage and salve the wound. I was in to see the doc yesterday. He said another week and the bandage can come off. I knew the men would begin to wonder and grumble. If I'm to get along here, I got to be one of them."

"Don't you start telling me how to run my ranch," Jed said angrily.

"Nobody is telling you," Handy said. "It's just that sometimes things get out of hand without anyone's intention. You've done considerable for me which I'll not forget but I don't belong here and everybody knows it. I'll pick up the things you've given me and go down to the bunkhouse now with Jake. He can find work that I can handle so at least it will look like I'm busy. Your men have been loyal to you and worked hard, like I heard about the night of that storm and after. You can't risk losing them. You need them worse than you need me."

Jake had watched Handy closely. No expression showed in his eyes or on his bearded, dark face.

It was apparent Jed did not like to have his decisions challenged and his lined face was tight but he yielded. "All right," he told Handy, "if that's the way you want it."

"It's the way it has to be," Handy said.

Jed swung to Jake. "He'll be along shortly. I want to talk to him. Just take things easy with him for a while."

"Sure," Jake said, looking at Handy as if he were taking his measure. "I'll be waiting for you in my room. It's at the end of the bunkhouse." He clomped out.

At the desk, Jed shook his head. "You shouldn't of done that," he told Handy. "It's my word that's law here."

"I know, and I didn't want to cross you," Handy said, "but Jake was right about the men."

"Maybe so," Jed grumbled. He left the desk and went to the gun cabinet. A gun belt with holster was hanging on a peg. He took it out and the Walker Colt. "Put it on," he said.

Handy was dumfounded. "I appreciate the loan," he said, taking the gun and belt.

"It's yours," Jed said, "and the Henry when you can sit a horse."

"Jed, I can't. . . ." Handy began.

"The hell you can't," Jed said gruffly. "Another thing, you get down to that wheel every night after supper and fire off a few rounds. Anybody shoots like you don't want to get out of practice."

Handy couldn't find the words he wanted to say. Gruff and ornery as Jed could be, he was soft inside and considerate of a man. "Got a thong?" he asked, buckling on the belt.

"Why, sure," Jed said, looking curiously at Handy. He reached in a desk drawer and brought out a strip of rawhide.

Handy set the holster low on his thigh and tied it so it

slanted forward. When he dropped the gun in the holster, the butt was back for an easy, fast draw. Jed was smiling when Handy glanced at him. Handy grinned back. He knew he'd fixed the holster in the gunman's position. "It's just that it's quicker this way," he explained.

"I know," Jed said heartily. "It's fine, just fine." He hesitated as if he were going to say something more and Handy waited expectantly. Abruptly, Jed shook his head and muttered, "It better wait."

Handy was puzzled by Jed's attitude and curious about the references Jed and Jake had made earlier but did not ask the questions that were growing in his mind. Instead, he said, "Will you tell Nan what has happened? Tell her I'm sorry. I hope she'll understand."

Jed frowned but he nodded his head.

Big Jake's room at the end of the bunkhouse was a rat hole. It was a boarded-off cubicle along one side. A narrow aisle extended beyond his door to another door at the back. The sour and dirty room smelled of whiskey and tobacco. In a corner three empty Double Stamp Bourbon bottles nested in a wad of soiled clothes. On an upended wooden cartridge case a tin lid was overflowing with stained butts. Another cartridge case nailed to the wall was stuffed with shirts and biscuits. Two whiskey bottles shoved their necks through a jumble of jackets and Levis. A gray blanket was crumpled on a cot like the one in the lean-to and Jake sat on it.

"I see you're heeled," Jake said, staring at the holstered gun. "Jed loan it to you?"

"Yep." Handy decided it would be better not to mention the gun was a gift.

"The men don't carry iron when they're at headquarters," Jake growled, "but I guess it's different with you."

"If that's the rule, I'll take it off," Handy said. What did Jake mean, different with him?

"No," Jake said. "Jed wants you to pack it, you do like Jed says. Reckon you'd feel naked without it."

"I would," Handy admitted.

"Thought so." Jake chewed his cheek inside his beard. "What else can you do, besides shoot?"

"Ride, rope, break a bronc, throw a steer." Handy looked hard at Jake. He was annoyed at the continued reference to guns and shooting and said coldly, "Shoot a bear or man at a thousand yards or fifty feet."

"You'll do," Jake said grudgingly. "Until you're able to pull your weight, I'll let you off with light work like cleaning out the barn. Today you can clean the bunkhouse."

"That's squaw's work," Handy spluttered angrily. It was beneath a self-respecting cow poke's dignity.

"Don't rile me," Jake warned. "The squaws been so busy tending you, they ain't had time for it. You'll find the broom, mop and bucket beside the door. Start with my room. There's a pit out back for slop and trash."

Handy decided the only thing he could do was put the best face on it however disagreeable the job Jake assigned him. It was true he owed them all. He grinned and said, "Sure, Jake."

Jake showed him a bunk with a stained hair mattress by the door and gave him scrubbed thin Levis and a blue denim shirt. "You can use these for work clothes." He went across to another bunk and pulled off blankets and a filthy feather pillow. He pitched the pillow to Handy. "Understand you got to have this to sit and sleep on."

Handy tossed the pillow out the door. "I'll burn it before I sleep on it," he said.

"Suit yourself," Jake said and shrugged, "only don't go saying I didn't offer you it." His blue-green eyes studied Handy for a minute and then he said harshly, "There's one more thing, Southern. You stay off from Nan. Ain't fitting one like you should so much as talk to her. You don't go near the white house, not less Jed sends for you." He stomped out.

Handy held back his temper although his stomach was churning. Big Jake was the price he'd have to pay if he wanted to stay on the Lazy J but he knew it was only a matter of time until there'd be a showdown. He pulled off the clothes Jed had given him and got into the work clothes. They must have been

Big Jake's because they fit. He didn't like the idea of wearing Jake's castoffs but they were clean. When he'd hung his gun belt on a peg beside his bunk, he spread his blankets and began carting bottles and cans, which he filled with cigarette butts, to the slop hole at the back. He'd finished sweeping and was mopping Jake's room when Roy slumped against the door jamb.

"Told you to live it up while you could," he slurred. "That Jake, ain't he the one? Don't know how he does it but he always finds the right job for everybody."

Handy managed a grin. "Nothing sorrier in this world than a broken-down poke," he said pleasantly.

"Pa sure lost money when he bet on you," Roy said.

This angered Handy and he snapped, "I know what I owe. He'll get full value when I'm able to hold my own."

"Sure, bulldogging a broom," Roy sneered. He started to leave and turned back. His eyes were smoldering. "They was mighty good to you up at the house and you took advantage of them. Now you're here where you should of been right from the start, there's no call for you to push yourself on Nan no more. Only reason she treated you decent was she was sorry for you. Don't go near her." He ground out his cigarette on the clean floor and tromped out.

When Handy went to the cook shack at noon, he'd finished the bunkhouse but he was tired. There were only half a dozen hands including Roy, Ron and Rod at the table. He sat next to Roy because the dishes of food were bunched in front of the brothers. No one offered him anything. He had to name each item and ask for it. It was an effort but he kept his voice calm.

Roy, Ron and Rod put their heads together and guffawed. Roy said to his brothers, "Reckon we can fix up a saddle to fit the mop handle."

The brothers laughed uproariously at this and the three hands across the table snickered.

Handy spooned his stew and ignored them although he was fuming.

"Maybe he could put his brand on the bucket," Ron suggested.

They thought that was very funny, too, and one of the hands, a little red-headed man, laughed aloud.

Handy mopped up the last of his stew with a slab of bread and gulped his coffee.

"The squaw work's done in the bunkhouse," Rod said. "Maybe we could find something puny for him to do this afternoon to earn his keep."

Handy picked up his tin plate and cup and flatware. He looked narrowly at each of the brothers in turn when he stood. "I take my orders from Big Jake," he said in a voice that rang like iron struck with a sledge and carried his dishes to the kitchen in the silence that followed him.

"No need fo' you do, Li Shu do," the small Chinaman protested.

Although Handy had heard Li Shu mentioned often he had not seen the cook before. He had saffron skin and almond-shaped eyes and wore his hair in a queue as did all the Chinamen Handy had seen, but Li Shu possessed something different. It was a broad, white, warm smile.

He smiled now and said, "Glad you out of bed."

"Thanks, Li Shu," Handy told him. "So am I."

Handy heard Big Jake's voice in the dining room and looked out. He was talking with Roy, Ron and Rod. "You boys," he was saying, "I want you up on the north range. I want a herd count. I think we're being rustled. We got few 'nough head left without losing them to rustlers." He saw Handy in the kitchen doorway and a slow smile parted his beard. "Was wondering what to do with you this afternoon. Seeing you there just give me a idea. You stay right where you are and lend a hand to Li Shu. You can carry out the slop pails, do the dishes, mop down the cook shack."

Everyone except Li Shu laughed.

Handy chuckled and asked the cook, "Got an apron that will fit me?"

Li Shu shook his head so vigorously that his queue swung like a pendulum from shoulder to shoulder. "Not light. You sick fella. Not light anytime you do Li Shu job. I get you pillow. You sit and lest."

"And get cheated out of your hot biscuits and tasting the food you're cooking for supper?" Handy laughed. "I'm going to be right in the kitchen with you. Since I got back on my feet again, I've developed a mighty hearty appetite."

"Ho-ho," Li Shu said and spread his grin across his face. "You sly fella."

Big Jake looked like someone had just topped his straight with a flush and the others stopped laughing.

Handy sluiced out the shack and carried out the slop and ate his way through the afternoon. Li Shu tittered each time he brought another cup of coffee and hot biscuits or a piece of pie to Handy. He'd brought Handy his pillow from the lean-to. "Missy Nan say, you take to bunkhouse," he told Handy, who was trying to put her out of his mind. He didn't like being told, but he, himself, had already made up his mind to stay away from her. He was relieved that Jake had sent the brothers to the north range. They hadn't liked it but they'd ridden out and would be gone a few days. With them out of the way, Handy hoped he could establish better relations with the other men.

When the crew started drifting in for supper, Handy, who'd not stopped eating all afternoon, buckled on the gun belt, tied down the holster and walked toward the haystack. He was tired and his butt wound felt tight. It made him limp a little.

He gave the wheel a turn, stepped off twenty-five paces, whirled, drawing and firing. He did this four more times, starting with his back to the wheel. He was examining the cards, all hit shots although only one was dead center, when Nan surprised him.

"Handy," she said softly. She was beside him, dressed as usual in shirt and Levis. Her eyes looked especially soft and warm.

"Nan," he exclaimed and felt his heart jump. "What are you doing here?"

"I heard the firing and knew it was you." She was prettier

when she frowned as she did now. "We were going to have a picnic today."

He shook his head. "I know. I'm sorry. It had to be this way."

"But why?"

"Didn't your father tell you?" he asked gently. His chest was beginning to pain at her nearness. "It was the way I knew it would be. The men resented my being at the white house and Big Jake and Jed were arguing about me this morning."

"I was angry when Pa told me," she said.

"I know."

"It's going to make a difference, isn't it?" Her eyes were pleading.

"I'm afraid so, Nan. I have no right. I don't even own the clothes on my back. The way things are, I can't do more than say 'Howdy' when I pass you."

"And that's all you're going to do?" She usually sounded breathless but now she was subdued.

"Yes, Nan. It's all I can do. Anything else would not be fair to you."

Angrily, she burst out, "It isn't fair for you to ignore me."

"Believe me, Nan," he said earnestly, "I could never ignore you. But the circumstances prevent our being together as we have been."

"You're making me miserable, Handy," she said and there was a catch in her voice.

"I am truly sorry," he said painfully. "Perhaps it would be better if I'd go away."

"No," she cried. After a moment she seemed to realize what she'd said and what her protest meant. "Where would you go and what would you do?"

"I'd manage. I think that's the answer."

"Don't make me beg," she said woefully. "At the least, stay here."

"Yes," he agreed. "It will hurt but I'll stay. I owe."

Suddenly she reached up, brought his face to hers and kissed him on the lips. She swirled and ran toward the house. She was sobbing.

◎◎◎◎◎◎◎◎◎◎◎◎

# CHAPTER XI

◎◎◎◎◎◎◎◎◎◎◎◎◎

Nan left the ranch the next morning. Handy learned about it from Li Shu.

"Missy Nan go by Livaton," the Chinaman told him soberly when Handy cleared the cluttered table of breakfast dishes. Jake had assigned him to the cook shack again.

Nan had mentioned that she had cousins in Riverton, her mother's people, Handy remembered. He felt an acute sense of loss but he decided she had done the best thing possible under the circumstances. The visit would avoid any chance meeting which would be painful to her after the way she'd bared her emotions the day before. Her absence would also relieve the mounting tension over her with Jake, Roy, Rod and Ron.

"How long will she be gone?" Handy asked.

"Don' know." Li Shu did not have a smile in him this morning. "Only know she not happy. Full Moon say she cly all time. Mista Jed dlive she by Gleen Liva."

Handy considered whether he should take the opportunity while she was away to drift on. He decided against it. It was not the considerable difficulty he would have, penniless and horseless, that determined him to stay on but a genuine desire to be near Nan although she'd be forever out of reach. That was the real reason, but he told himself he had to remain until his debt to Jed and Jake was repaid and he had a horse.

When Jake came in at noon, he pulled Handy from the cook shack and put him to work cleaning the outhouses. He gave him a pair of boots and ragged Levis. Handy gagged and retched in the hot, confined pits. He hauled off a hundred buckets to the ditch he'd dug. When he'd purified the holes with lime, he went to the river and scrubbed the boots with lime and himself with lye soap. He burned the Levis he'd worn.

Although he wore the work clothes Jake had given him at supper that night, the men made a great show of moving down the bench away from him. They didn't press it too far with words. He was wearing the low-slung gun belt and he could feel his eyes were steely.

Jed came down to the haystack when Handy started firing. He watched silently while Handy did his turnabout—drew and fired five times.

"You got your hand and eye back in one hell of a hurry," he said approvingly when Handy plunked the pip with every shot.

"Hip's a little stiff, wound still tightens it up," Handy said and reloaded. "I'm not turning as fast as I should."

"It'll limber up," Jed said. He lighted his face with a smile. "Main thing is, you're shooting straight and doing it the hard way." He paused and his smile became a frown. "Hear Jake's been riding roughshod on you."

Handy laughed. "I can take anything he throws my way."

"So I hear, but he's carrying it too far. I'll speak to him."

"No, Jed," Handy said quickly. "That would make things worse. Let me handle it my way. I can best him. He wants me to fuss. When I don't, he looks foolish to the men. He'll ease off soon as he learns."

Jed smiled and nodded his head. After a pause, he said, "Nan went to visit cousins in Riverton this morning."

"Li Shu told me."

"She didn't want to go. Any idea why she did?"

It was hard but Handy said it. "She and I spent too much time together. She realized I wasn't seemly company for her."

"She has a head," Jed said somberly. "I like you, son, but the way you earn your living, you're not the kind of man for her."

Handy didn't resent the remark, coming from Jed. Quietly, he said, "I'd come to the same conclusion."

Roy, Ron and Rod came back from the north range. They reported a head count on that graze of 250 cows.

"That's about right," Jake said. "I was certain the rustlers was getting them."

Handy, who was digging post holes for a holding pen near the corral, had the idea Jake had sent the brothers on a wild-goose chase to get them out of his hair. He wished Jake would think of something else to keep them away. Now that they were back, they amused themselves jibing at Handy.

"He handles that spade like a regular sodbuster," Roy said.

"I thought he was a sheep dipper, the way he handled the mop bucket," Ron said, "but the pokes tell me he's not a sheep dipper. He's a honey diver."

"Ask him," Rod said, "how does he like working for a living after having breakfast brought to him in bed."

"Squaw work, all squaw work," Roy sneered.

When he paid no attention and the sport dulled, the three of them rode into Green River. Handy knew the day was approaching when he'd have to settle the score with them as well as Jake. The way he felt about them, completely contemptuous, he was ready to take on all three at the same time. They returned from Green River near midnight roaring drunk and awakened everyone in the bunkhouse with their caterwauling. Jake doused them with a bucket of water and cuffed them to their room.

Handy's relationship with Jake and the brothers was restrained. There wasn't one of them he didn't want to smash with his fists and feel bones crunch but he clenched his teeth and went quickly about his business. He obeyed Jake's orders and exchanged no words with the boys. Jake he could understand. The man was naturally mean. Also, he was the foreman and expected a day's work from everyone, which he did not consider he was getting from Handy. The brothers were plain shiftless and worthless. Although Jed had turned them out of the house, they still assumed their positions as sons and heirs of the owner. No one was deferential to them but no one crossed them, either. They were tolerated in uneasy silence.

Handy had hoped he might form some friendships with the others but, while they were civil enough, they withdrew when he approached. Perhaps it was the obvious disfavor in which Jake held him that made them wary, or it may have been the gun he wore. Jake had explained it by telling the men that he was a gunman, which was so ridiculous it made Handy laugh but it also showed the length to which Jake would go to make life miserable. Handy became a loner and the only real interests he had were occasional talks with Jed and his target practice.

Although the tasks Jake gave Handy were the most unpleasant he could find, most were manual labor and Handy was grateful for this. The weakness was gone from his arms and legs and his muscles were hard and firm. He'd never be fat but he'd filled out his frame with tough lean flesh. Big Jake carried more weight but Handy looked more durable. A thick membrane had grown over the hole in his buttock and his hip was no longer stiff. The one thing that remained from his ordeal was the bare patch of skull bone where hair would never grow. He still kept a pad over it.

He missed seeing Nan, riding off from the corral or weeding in her flower garden behind the house. He'd resigned himself to a passing "Howdy" relationship but he still wanted her at the ranch. A thought seized and possessed him when two weeks passed and she did not return. She'd met some eligible man at Riverton and would marry him and never come back. The idea dismayed him.

She returned during the third week. Jed brought her from Green River in the surrey. Watching from the bunkhouse, Handy thought she looked frail. Immediately he began to worry that she'd been sick and that was why she'd come back to the Lazy J. He wanted to go to the house and ask about her but knew he could not.

It was Jake who went to the kitchen door carrying a trinket, a gaudy bauble of glass and feathers in the form of a bird. Going to the back door was a privilege Jake, as range boss, accorded himself and one which Jed tolerated, although, except when summoned to the office, Handy did not think Jake entered the house. Hadn't Jed thrown out his own sons? Handy saw Nan at the door talking briefly with Jake and then the hulking black-bearded man stomped back toward the bunk-house. There was a dark look to him, as if his reception and gift had not been all he'd hoped.

Handy waited until Jake was in his room and then went down to the haystack. He wished without hope Nan might hear him firing and come down but was certain she would not. He had explained the circumstances that kept them apart and she had gone to Riverton to be away from him. His turn, draw and fire was not so accurate as usual and he missed one of the cards completely on his first five rounds. He was facing the wheel, reloading, when, unexpectedly, Nan was standing beside him.

"Hello, Handy," she said. Her voice sounded too vigorous and gay, as if she were forcing it. Her face did seem pale and her eyes too bright. She was wearing an apron with deep pockets over a pale green dress and she was holding her hands behind her back.

"Hello, Nan." He could not bring himself to "Howdy, ma'am" her. "I'm glad to see you again."

"Thank you for that, Handy." The pitch of her voice dropped to normal although there was a catch in it and it was not breathless. "I brought you something."

When she showed her hands, he saw she was holding a hair-piece, a magnificent, long golden-haired wig. The hair was the same color as Nan's.

"Nan!" he exclaimed, taking the hairpiece and stroking it. The hair was silky soft and gleamed with a sheen. Inside was a white pad. From its position it would cover his skull where it was bare. "I don't know what to say or how to say it. Dear Nan."

"You just did, Handy," she said softly. "Mine needed thinning, anyway."

"It's your hair?" he gasped.

A smile trembled on her lips and then she said, very business-like, "I talked with Dr. Bainbridge. He agreed a wig was a good idea. The pad is antiseptic and stitched into place so it can be changed. A squaw at Riverton took two or three strands of hair at a time and knotted them into place in a soft leather skull-cap."

"Your own hair," he repeated. He could not find words. He would be wearing Nan's own hair. No knight in armor ever possessed such a favor from his lady. He removed his hat, meaning to set the hairpiece on his head.

"Not yet," she said. Her eyes were dancing now. "We've some adjustments to make if it's to fit proper. Sit down."

Obediently, he hunkered. She brought a comb and scissors from a pocket of her apron. He had been letting his hair grow long, meaning to brush it back over the skull bone. She combed it forward and began to snip. The nearness of her when she brushed his shoulder, the fragrance of her when she touched his face made him dizzy. He sat unprotesting while she cut off all his hair and then she stepped back, considered and snipped some more close to the skull. Then she took the hairpiece from his hands and adjusted it carefully. The hairpiece smelled of her and, running his hands back from the top of his head, felt of her.

"Handy," she exclaimed excitedly and delightedly, "it worked just the way I wanted. You are handsome."

He stood and she reached into the other pocket of her apron for a mirror. "Look."

Handy was speechless. He was fascinated by the stranger with golden shoulder-length hair who stared back at him. He saw, too, that as his face had filled out all the hard lines had disappeared. His blue eyes and the golden hair made his bronzed cheeks look even darker.

"I don't know me, Nan," he said simply. "You have given me the greatest gift."

"Handsome Handy," was all she said, but her eyes were big and shining. She looked at him intently and then she was in his arms and he was kissing her.

Abruptly she stepped away and looked to the west. The sun was disappearing behind Church Butte. "I'll be late for supper," she said, and without another word or look, she ran toward the house. This time she was not sobbing.

Handy stroked Nan's hair a dozen times. He was deeply in love with her. He did not yet know how but he meant to marry Nan.

He removed the hairpiece, folded it carefully and put it in his pocket before he placed the old pad under his hat and started slowly back toward the bunkhouse.

# CHAPTER XII

Handy was mending bob wire on the fence that bounded head-quarters the next afternoon when Jed squatted beside him. "How's the sitter?" Jed asked.

"Tough enough to ride a steer," Handy said and laughed. He'd been feeling good enough to ride a cloud since the evening before with Nan and was impatiently awaiting the supper hour because he was certain she'd be at the haystack as soon as he started firing. "I was fixing to tell Jake tonight I'm fit to ride the range."

"Good," Jed said enthusiastically. He climbed back on his heels and stood facing Handy. There seemed to be a twinkle in the old man's bright eyes. "But we'll not push into things until we're certain for sure." He reached into his pocket and brought out five cartwheels, which he held in his palm to Handy. "That's a draw on your first month's salary. We'll find you a horse and saddle. Ride into town and see how it goes."

Handy hesitated. He didn't want to go to Green River. He wanted to see Nan.

"You got it coming," Jed urged. "You showed yourself a man. It's been a long dry spell. Get a noseful. Come back when you're ready or broke."

Handy thought briefly on it. Jed was being thoughtful again, and considerate. He had a right to know whether Handy was in condition to start working his real job as cowboy. Jed would tell Nan he'd sent him into town. She'd understand. "Sure," he said with a grin. "And thanks."

Jed found a saddle on the rack worn enough to be comfortable and cinched it on a mustang old enough not to get notions. He hung a rope on the apple and gave Handy a Bowie knife. "Hang it on your belt," he said. "There's times when you need it."

Handy went to the bunkhouse and changed into his good clothes—Ron's discards. He was uncertain about the hairpiece but no one in town knew him and it was Friday so none of the crew from the Lazy J would be there. Saturday was the night the hands hurrahed the town. He set the wig on his clipped head and clapped the flat-crowned black hat over it. Abundant hair flowed from it about his shoulders. The men had joked some when they'd seen his cropped hair that morning. He'd silenced them quickly. "Doc's orders. He's afraid of scalp infection." He also wore the gun belt with the holster tied forward on his thigh so the butt slanted and was within easy drawing reach.

It was a warm, bright late-summer afternoon and the blue sky was shining. It was good to have a horse under him again and his chewed buttock did not chafe or ache in the saddle. Now and then he'd lift the mustang from a trot to a gallop for a short distance, testing himself. Trotting or galloping, the horse had a good gait and Handy hoped Jake would give him this horse to ride the range. It was strange, he thought. He assumed he'd be riding the range, and when he'd spoken of it neither Jed nor Jake had contradicted him, but neither had ever directly discussed with him the nature of his duties. He'd be in the saddle, that he knew, one of the hands, but there had been many indirect indications that his work was not to follow the routine of the ordinary cowboy.

Green River was snoozing on a quiet afternoon when Handy rode in. Four horses, all paints, were tied at the hitch rail in front of the Trail's End saloon. A few women carrying parasols against the sun toed the boardwalk. A black mongrel yipped and slunk away from three boys who pelted it with stones. An empty wagon stood in front of E. Higginbotham's, Genl. Mdse. Handy tied up at the rail outside Doc Bainbridge's prim white cottage and stepped into the office.

There were no patients. The doc was sitting behind his flat-topped desk with an opened medical book under his hand but he was asleep. His seamed face looked care-worn and tired. He always looked tired, Handy recalled. He turned and started to walk quietly out when the doc called him back.

"What's the matter? You change your mind?" The doc's voice was edgy.

Handy turned and the doc stared at him over the tops of his spectacles. "Bejesus!" he exclaimed. "I didn't recognize you from the rear with all that hair around your shoulders. Come here, man, take off your hat. Let me have a look at you."

Handy smiled broadly and removed the hat. The doc shook his head. "She did it. She did it proud. I told her the idea of a wig was good but I had no idea it would turn out like this. You're a new man, Handy." He came around his desk. "Let me see." He removed the hairpiece. When he'd examined the pad and Handy's skull, he said, "That's Nan's own hair, isn't it?"

Handy's face felt hot and he nodded his head without speaking.

"Nothing to be ashamed of," the doc said briskly. "Not a man in Wyoming Territory wouldn't give a month's pay to wear Nan's hair. I'll fix up half a dozen sterile pads for you to take back. Nan can change them every week or so." He paused and glanced curiously at Handy's cropped hair. "Who cut it?"

Handy's face flushed again. He mumbled, "Nan."

The doc chuckled. He asked, "You ride in?"

"Yep," Handy said. He held out his hand for Nan's hair and replaced it on his head. "No trouble."

"Let's have a look."

Handy dropped his Levis and lay on his stomach on the cot. The doc probed the hollow in his cheek, poking his forefinger roughly against the new membrane. "Hurt?" he asked.

"Not a mite," Handy said truthfully.

"You're fit," the doc said as Handy buttoned up. Doc sized him up and down, grasped his arms and legs, felt his shoulders. "Broad as an ax handle and strong as an ox. Not a thing you can't do and better than most. Downright miracle, considering.

Better than most," he repeated and laughed. "Especially with that hair."

The doc made up sterile pads, packaged them in oil skin and tied them tightly. "Have Nan keep them for you," he said.

Handy laid two cartwheels on the doc's desk. "I'll be paying you what I can every month, when I draw my pay," he said.

The doc pushed the silver dollars back to Handy. "Jed's already took care of all of it," he said.

The special consideration Jed was giving him was more than passing strange, Handy thought. It was almost as if the tough old rancher wanted him under obligation. It wasn't Jed's place to pay his doctor bills.

Handy put the pads in a saddlebag and rode down the dusty street. He tied up at the Busy Bee—Eats. The steak and fried potatoes his two bits bought did not compare with Li Shu's but were worth the price, the way the pretty girl behind the counter kept staring at him.

After his early supper, he stomped the boardwalk staring into the windows at calico and tinware and looking at the people. It was a quiet time of day and not many were about. He stepped into E. Higginbotham's and bought a plain beige kerchief for Nan. It cost him the same as his meal, which lay heavy on his stomach. He did not stable the mustang at the livery. He had an idea he'd be returning to the ranch that night. There was no doubt about it, he thought and chuckled. He knew damned well he was going back. He wanted to watch Nan's face when she saw the kerchief.

When the sun went down, he rode to the Trail's End and tied up. The four paints had been replaced by three roans. The rancid odor of whiskey and beer and old tobacco smoke in the murky saloon almost drove him back on the street. It was a low-down, stinking hole. Four men were at the bar. They looked like storekeepers in their stiff-collared shirts and vests. Three men were seated under a coal-oil lamp that spilled yellow light on the green felt of a gaming table. They wore flat-crowned black hats like Handy's and checked vests over silver piped shirts. The game they were playing was matador, with dominoes, but a poker deck and chips were on the table. All three looked at Handy, hopefully, he thought. He shook his head, stepped to the bar and a player closed an end with a two-bone for a seven.

Handy ordered a glass of beer. It had been months since he'd taken a drink of whiskey and he did not trust himself. The unaccustomed tingle of the beer was pleasantly bitter at his first swallow. He upended the glass at the next gulp and ordered another. This he drank slowly, watching the domino players. The men were not interested in their game, only passing the time in the hope someone with coin in his poke would come in.

Handy built a smoke and finished his beer. He was ready to ride back. He'd had a bad supper but he had seen the doctor. The beer had tasted good but he'd had enough. The saloon depressed him. He didn't know what else he'd expected to find in town. He turned to leave when the batwings swung and Roy, Ron and Rod stalked in from the night. Handy quickly turned his back to them. He didn't want them to see him in his hairpiece. It would only provide them with new ammunition to fire at him. They stormed down the bar and ordered whiskey.

Handy knew he should slip out but he'd heard talk at the bunkhouse of how the brothers carried on in town and he was curious. He ordered another beer and kept his back to them, listening. They called for a bottle of Old Crow and carried it to the gaming table.

"With us, there's six," Roy slurred to the domino players. "Five-card stud?"

"Suits us," one of the men said.

The brothers pulled out chairs and the play started. The stakes were high but not unreasonable, two bits a chip. Each had bought a $25 stack. Rod and Ron managed to keep their losses low but Roy bet wildly and lost steadily.

"The hell with this penny-ante game," he grumbled and poured another glass of whiskey. "Let's cash in and start again. Dollar a chip." He put a sneer in his voice. "Or is that too rich for your blood?"

"A dollar a chip," the banker said evenly. He was a cat-eyed critter.

Each man cashed in and laid out $100 for a new stack.

During the next hour, with the brothers intent on their bottle and cards, Handy turned and watched the play. The three of them were getting drunk and losing almost every hand. They usually stayed to the last card. The other men seemed to have some arrangement because by the time the last card was dealt, only one of them would be in the play. Handy suspected them of palming.

Ron and Rod had short stacks when Roy bet his last chips and waited for his card. He drew a six of clubs to a possible straight showing. The dealer gave himself a queen of hearts to make two pair up. He'd palmed the card and this time Handy had seen it. So had Roy.

"You palmed that card," Roy shouted, upsetting his chair when he jumped up. "I seen it."

"You saying I cheated?" The dealer was on his feet and he had a pepperbox derringer in his hand. The other two men were also up. All three wore gun belts. None of the brothers was armed.

Handy moved quietly along the bar until he was next to the table. His hand snaked out and he grasped the dealer's gun hand, bringing it up and behind his back. The man howled with pain and outrage. Handy had his Walker Colt in his fist covering the other two men.

"I say you cheated," he said and twisted the dealer's wrist. The derringer dropped to the floor. Handy released the wrist and clouted the man on the chin with his left fist. The dealer sank to his knees with his chin resting on the edge of the table. Handy glared at the banker. "I say the three of you cheated all night. Give the men their money, a hundred dollars each."

The banker snarled but he doled out the money. "We'll get you for this," he said.

The brothers scooped up their money and stared at Handy. Recognition was slowly showing in their bleary eyes.

"It's Handy," Rod finally said.

"Last time I saw him, he didn't have no hair," Ron said.

"We got to find out, who is his barber," Roy said.

Handy kept the three men at the table covered and did not look at the brothers. "Take your money and get out," he said. "Next time stay sober."

The brothers hooted and staggered through the batwings.

"Outside, you three," the barkeep shouted. He was holding a sawed-off shotgun. "Don't want no trouble."

"You heard him," Handy told the three men. "Out."

The three scowled fiercely at Handy and the one started to pick up his pepperbox. "Leave it," Handy told him and he did. The three left with dark backward looks at Handy. He scooped up the derringer, shoved it in his pocket and holstered his .44.

"Sorry," he told the red-faced beefy bartender. "Who are they?"

The barkeep put his shotgun behind the bar. "Never set eyes on them before," he said. His eyes slitted on Handy. "Never seen you before, neither."

"Handy Southern," he told the bartender. "Lazy J."

The barkeep took in Handy's heft and the way he wore his gun. "Guess you be the new man Jed been talking about. Bragging how you could shoot the eye out of a flea. You be the one crawled into town half dead."

Handy nodded.

The butcher-faced bardog poured half a glass of Old Crow. "It's on the house," he said, pushing it to Handy. "My name's Ralph. Knew them three was trouble when they come in. Don't know what they're up to. Just passing through, I hope." He came around the bar and looked over the swinging doors. "Rode off somewheres. I'd keep a eye out if I was you. They'll bushwhack you if they can find the chance." On the other side of the bar again, he said, "Anything you can do about them boys of Jed's? They're free spenders but always getting drunk, gaming and fighting. Must give Jed fits. Only thing they use their heads about, they don't carry iron. Never see a man before pull a gun on a man wasn't heeled."

Handy tossed off the whiskey. It found the beer in his stomach and lay there warm and pleasant. "Obliged," he said and left.

He rode slowly down the street. Although the only lights were the lanterns in the dozen saloons, there was a full moon and he could see into the cross streets. He discovered three roans at the hitch rail in front of the Stockman's Bar. Over the batwings, he saw the three men who'd cheated the brothers at a table in the back playing cards with three pokes. He rode on past the Golden West and Bald Steer. There was little activity and he found no Lazy J horses anywhere. He did not think the boys had gone back to the ranch.

He told himself he was behaving like a bronc with a burr under his blanket to go running around town searching for Roy, Ron and Rod. It should give him satisfaction if they landed in a patch of grief. But they only passed it on to Jed.

When he came to the Busy Bee, he saw a man behind the counter. He went in for a cup of coffee.

"I'm a stranger," he told the bald-headed man who served him. "Any fancy houses hereabouts?"

The counterman took his measure and finally drawled, "It's the Bohunk's you'd be wanting. Bohemian Belle's. Not what it used to be when the stage come through and this was the division point, but it's still the best there is. Down to the end of Main Street and north. You can't miss it. It's a two-story wood house with a porch. Only two-story house in that end of town."

Handy found the house without difficulty. Three mustangs with the Lazy J brand were hitched in front of it. Lamps were lighted at a downstairs window and two of the upstairs windows. Handy built a smoke and hooked a leg around the pommel while he thought on what to do. He couldn't very well slam on in and order the boys back to the ranch, but on the other hand, he was afraid they were in no condition to get home by themselves and there were the three men from the card table to consider. If those disgruntled gamblers came across them, they'd knock them silly and take all their money if they didn't kill them. Handy reined in to the shadow of a cottonwood and smoked two more cigarettes before the boys stumbled onto the porch.

Ron and Rod were supporting Roy. The two of them swayed along the board walkway while Roy's boot toes scraped the wood. Halfway to the hitching posts, Rod collapsed and he and Ron lay facedown without moving. Roy found his feet in a widening circle as he tried to locate his brothers. He carried a bottle in his hand. He hoisted it to his mouth, and when he'd emptied it, tossed it into the bush and lay down.

Handy ground-reined the mustang and uncurled the rope. He hoisted Roy across his shoulders and carried him to the first horse. He bellied him across the saddle, cut a length of rope, tied his arms and legs and cinched him in. For good measure, he threw a hitch around the apple. He did the same for the others. He didn't mind carrying the dead weight. It was cutting the good throwing rope that bothered him.

He strung the three horses, with their loads like bags of grain, together with the reins and, holding the leather for Roy's lead horse, started walking them back to the ranch. He traveled a side street west until he reached the edge of town and then trailed crosscountry a good half mile from the road. He kept turning in his saddle and looking back to see whether the three men from the card game were following. There was no sight of them and although he knew they were too drunk to hear he roundly read out the three sons of Jed for their stupidity and the burden they must be to him.

It was nearing midnight when the horses crested a hill and Handy looked down the slope to the sleeping ranch and the shrunken river beyond rippling in the moonlight. For a few minutes, the strange train was silhouetted against the bright night sky and then they were in the shadow of the hill. Handy led the horses to the bunkhouse and, one by one, carried the boys to their cots in their back room beyond Jake's. He dropped each and left him. He made no effort to pull off the boots.

When he'd racked the saddles and turned the horses into the pasture, he undressed and tucked the hairpiece into the pocket of his Levis before he stretched out on his own bunk.

◎◎◎◎◎◎◎◎◎◎◎◎◎◎

# CHAPTER XIII

◎◎◎◎◎◎◎◎◎◎◎◎◎◎

Nan hadn't been able to sleep that night.

She hadn't heard firing at the haystack and had asked her Pa at supper if Jake had sent Handy away on some chore.

"Nope," Jed said and chuckled. "I did. Gave him some on his salary so he could go to town and pour some whiskey in him. Man needs to loosen up now and then."

"Did he ride?" she asked excitedly.

"He sure did. Took off at a gallop and there was no daylight showing."

She was delighted he was fully mended and could ride again. It meant they could ride together in the early evenings and on Sundays.

After supper, she bridled her pony and went for a canter in the golden sunset. It was a glorious early evening and she took the road to Green River. She hoped Handy might remember that he'd kissed her the evening before and decide to return to the ranch. When the blue in the sky started to turn to purple, she reined about and went back toward the Lazy J at a walk. She still hoped Handy might come up with her.

It was Big Jake she encountered. Black Jake, she thought of him. She'd never liked him, and since that day he'd suddenly appeared at her door while she was in bed ill and ordered her not to see Handy, she'd mistrusted and resented him. It seemed to her he cast a black shadow on everyone who was near him. He pulled his buckskin around and rode beside her. She lifted Little Sister to a trot.

"Been looking for somebody?" Jake asked, keeping his horse beside her.

"Who would I look for out here?" she asked distantly.

"Dunno. This ain't usually the time or place you ride."
When she made no comment, he went on, "You seen that no-
count Southern since you come back?"

"What business is it of yours if I have?" she flared.

"I only got what's best for you in mind." He sounded angry.
"I warned you before, stay away from him. He's no good for
you." He snorted. "Anyway, you won't see him tonight or tomorrow neither. Your Pa gave him five dollars and he's in town
getting drunk and Lord knows what else."

She bit her lip and kicked her pony into a gallop. Jake
matched her gait.

"You don't believe me, ask your Pa," Jake shouted. "He's a
gunman, a hired killer."

He pulled up and it was a moment before she heard him
start for town at a dead run.

Jake was spiteful, mean and hateful, she told herself. Handy
was a gentleman come to poor circumstances through no fault
of his own. He was gentle and kind and honorable. Not once
had he made an untoward move. It was she who brazenly had
taken the initiative.

When she'd stabled Little Sister she had a cup of coffee with
her Pa and did not ask him whether Handy was a gunman.
The idea was preposterous. Yet the doubt had been planted
and was sprouting. She could not sleep when she went to bed
so she lighted the lamp and took up the *Lady of the Lake*. But
Sir Walter Scott did not hold her interest as usual. She kept
thinking about Handy. It was all right if he wanted to go to
town and have some drinks. All men did things like that, although after the kiss at the haystack it hurt a little that he preferred the sting of whiskey on his mouth to the taste of her
lips. He should have known that she'd come down when he
started his nightly target practice. And that was another thing
she did not understand, his obsession with guns and the constant routine of fast drawing and shooting. It was almost as if
he had to keep himself in form, sharp-honed and ready. The
way he wore his gun was strange. Most men wore guns at times

but she'd never seen a gun belt worn the way he wore his with the holster tied so the gun slanted forward.

She went back to bed and fretted and tossed for hours. Finally she got up and stood at her west window. The river was black with silver ripples in the moonlight and the night was beautifully quiet and calm. She thought a breath of air might soothe her worries and slipped a kimono over her nightgown. She went downstairs and out onto the front porch. Looking beyond the road and off to the hill, she was startled by an unusual sight. Against the sky she saw a rider leading three horses like a man with a pack train. Something was across the saddles of the horses he led. At that distance she could not tell who the rider was or what was on the saddles but the train was coming toward the ranch.

She ran to the corner of the porch and, standing against the house in the shadow, watched as the rider led the horses to the bunkhouse stoop. She gasped painfully when she saw the rider was Handy. He staggered as he lifted men to his shoulders from the saddles and carried them into the bunkhouse. Those men were her brothers. Handy had been in town carousing with them and they all were drunk.

It wasn't so much she minded what her brothers did to themselves. It was the way their behavior affected Pa. It had broken his heart when he'd had to turn them out of the house for their lazy, good-for-nothing ways and constant drinking. Now they had a companion to urge them on, a very bad companion if Jake was right.

Nan choked and fled to her room. She wept most of the night.

There was another witness to the nocturnal procession. It was Big Jake.

Smarting from Nan's rejection of his friendly overtures when he'd met her on the road, Jake had belted quite a few when he got to town. He'd finally worked his way to the Trail's End.

"Lazy J get the nights mixed, Jake?" Ralph, the brawny bardog, greeted him.

"What you mean by that?" Jake growled.

"You're the fifth one in from the Lazy J tonight," the barkeep said. "It ain't Saturday."

"Who else been in?" Jake asked suspiciously.

"Jed's three boys. That ain't uncommon. Then there was that new man, the one you picked off the street for dead." The bartender licked his lips and his little eyes gleamed. He placed a bottle of Double Stamp and a glass in front of Jake and leaned across the bar. "You should of been in when they were here, Jake. I thought there was going to be a shoot-out. They was playing poker with some strangers who was cheating. One of the strangers pulled a gun on Roy, and before you knew it that new man of yours had the gun out of his hand and knocked him flat with a left-hand blow whilst he covered the other two. He's a tough one. Made them give back the money and druv them out. Took a glass of whiskey in a gulp and went out hisself."

It gave Jake something to chew on in his black mood. He knew Southern was a gunman. If he'd thrown in with the boys and there was drinking, gaming, fighting and guns, all he'd told Nan had come true. The thing was, would she listen to him?

Thinking on how best to use his knowledge on the ride back sobered him although he formed no plan. He was not going to risk Nan's disdain by repeating what he'd already told her. He had turned his horse into the pasture and was walking toward the bunkhouse when he saw the rider leading three horses start down the hill. Curious, he stepped into the shadow of the barn and waited. Southern led the horses past him to the bunkhouse and carried in Jed's three boys one by one. Motion on the porch of the white house caught his eye and he saw a female figure that could be only Nan run into the house. She had observed the condition of Southern and her brothers. He did not think he needed to talk to her again.

# CHAPTER XIV

When Handy awakened the next morning the first thing he did was to check the pocket of his Levis for his hairpiece. He did it automatically and without thinking just as he'd always checked for his poke when he had one and his gun. The wig was not in his pocket. He was certain he'd put it in his pocket but he went through his shirt and work clothes and back through the pockets of his good Levis. The pepperbox was there and the silver. He got down on his knees and looked under the bunk. He shook the blankets. He pulled his boots from under the bunk and pawed through them. Nan's hair had disappeared.

He'd worn the hairpiece back to the ranch and placed it in his pocket. He was certain of that. He'd had one good-sized shot of whiskey on top of four or five glasses of beer but he had not been drunk. He clearly remembered every event of the evening and leading the brothers back to the ranch tied over their saddles. He remembered carrying them in and dumping them on their cots. He'd worn the hairpiece and he'd put it where he always kept it. He did not believe anyone could have been mean enough to steal it and as far as he knew no one knew about the wig except the brothers, if they remembered. The door to their room was closed but their snores rumbled through the bunkhouse.

Sick and aching at the loss of Nan's hair, he pulled on his Levis, tucked the legs into his boots and went outside to the bench to wash. He kept turning the miserable mystery of the wig over in his mind. Why would anyone take the wig and not the coins and pepperbox? The hairpiece was worthless except to him. The derringer had value both to a person and on the market. The only reason for taking the wig was downright, cussed spite. The only person who'd shown real resentment toward him was Big Jake. The range boss had given him every dirty job there was, had tried every way he knew to break him. Handy hadn't complained but he hadn't knuckled under and that brought bile to Jake's craw. Somehow or other, Jake must have learned about the wig. He might even have been up when Handy carried in the brothers and seen it. Jake had taken the hairpiece. It was the only answer.

Handy shook the water from his face and hands and clomped into the bunkhouse to face Jake down. He was raging. He was ready to take on Big Jake and fight until one of them was pulp.

In the bunkhouse the men were getting up. Some were half dressed. At the rear the door to the brothers' room opened and Ron and Rod in their rumpled, slept-in clothing staggered out. They were still drunk. They whooped and hollered and rolled down the aisle between the bunks, laughing uncontrollably and thumping each other's backs. Roy followed them. He was wearing Handy's wig and bellowing with mirth.

"Goldilocks," he shouted, pointing at Handy and howling. "Hey, Goldilocks."

Handy erupted down the aisle like a bronc coming out of the chute. He knocked Ron and Rod aside with swipes of his arms that sent them sprawling over men still in their bunks. Roy was still calling "Goldilocks" and roaring. Handy snatched the hairpiece from his head with his left hand and brought an uppercut to Roy's jaw from his knees. The blow lifted Roy from his boots and dropped him on the boards. He sat there a moment stunned and glassy-eyed. When he stood unsteadily, he seemed almost sober.

"Guess I had that coming," he said slowly. He turned and went back to his room. His brothers followed silently.

The bunkhouse was quiet until the door closed and then it exploded with noise like a wild bunch hurrahing a town. Big Jake was standing at his door. He grinned, a rare thing for him to do, and returned to his room. Handy put on his shirt and defiantly set the hairpiece on his head. No one laughed. He put on his hat and took the package with the scarf and the derringer to the white house. He did not expect to see Nan at this hour but he knew Jed would be up.

"Broke so soon?" Jed asked and made a sour face.

"Nope," Handy said. "The food in town isn't fit to eat. Doc Bainbridge told me you'd paid my bill. I want you to hold out five dollars from my salary every month until you're repaid. I appreciate all you've done for me but I don't want to be beholden more than necessary."

"We'll see about that," Jed said, poker-faced. "I see you got yourself some hair. Looks good."

Handy laid the package with the kerchief on the table. "Would you give this to Miss Nan with my compliments?" He laid the derringer beside it. "And this. She rides alone. I'd feel better if she was armed. There's strangers about."

Jed lifted the derringer and inspected it. "You didn't buy this. Not with the money you had."

"Nope. A gambler was pointing it in the wrong direction. He dropped it when he left."

"I won't ask how he come to leave his little gun behind," Jed said dryly, "and I'll give it to Nan." He clamped his jaw and his face went grim. He said harshly, "Like you said, strangers. Sheepmen and their herders and stinkers. Maybe gunmen." He looked hard at Handy. "They're pushing onto cattle range. Feeding off cow grass. It's coming, son. A damned war to keep what's ours by right."

"That why you've had me on the target, keeping my eye and hand in shape?" Handy asked. Things were beginning to fall into place.

"Mebbe."

"If it comes to a showdown, I'll not back off," Handy assured him. He'd fight if the sheepmen imported hired guns.

Jed's eyes took on a look of shrewdness. "I knew I could count on you," he said with what sounded like satisfaction. "I knew it from the start."

Jake sent Handy riding the draws alone that morning. He carried a spade. His task was simple enough. Bury any carcasses remaining from the flash flood that the coyotes hadn't finished.

"If there's just bones, don't bother with them," Jake said. "It's the rotting ones we got to get rid of. They draw flies and stink."

The gullies near headquarters had been cleared and Handy enjoyed the ride toward the north range. It was a pleasant, warm late-summer morning. The sky was an inverted blue-enameled bowl and the sun was bright and hot. There had been two showers in the past week and the hills showed green. He had the same mustang and saddle he'd used the afternoon before and Jed had brought down the Henry rifle in a boot when he'd seen Handy saddling up.

"You should of stayed in town like I said," he muttered. "Well, it's Saturday. Boys knock off along about five. Gives them a chance to spruce up, get into town before sundown. Take along the Henry. If you see any sheep or herders, shoot them."

Jed meant kill the sheep, not the herders, of course, Handy thought and chuckled. If the woollies were on deeded land, he'd shoot them without hesitating and bring one back to the cook shack for son-of-a-bitch stew.

It was late morning before Handy encountered the first putrefied carcass. Before tackling it, he reined off downstream and boiled coffee in the pot Li Shu had given him. After he'd eaten biscuits and jerky, he built a smoke and contemplated the river and the hills. This was a pleasant valley, a place where a man could be content. He'd not discussed salary with Jed or Jake but he supposed his wages would amount to $15 a month. At that figure he didn't see how he ever could think of marrying Nan. It would take most of a year to repay Jed for the doctor bill. Another $5 a month for tobacco, an occasional glass of beer and necessities. He should put aside $5 a month toward a horse and saddle. After a year he might have clothing and all he needed and could start to save $10 each time he was paid, $120 a year. It would be eight years before he could consider buying land, a few head of cattle and start building up a herd of his own. Even then he'd have nothing to offer Nan except the prospect of a dozen years of back-breaking work, if she waited that long for him, which he doubted.

There was an alternative. He owned the land at Fort Benton in Montana Territory. He was known there. At the end of a year he could return and, possibly, borrow enough from the bank to rebuild. It would take time but it looked like his only hope, if Nan would wait and if she would leave Wyoming Territory and her father.

His chances seemed mighty slim.

Disposing of the carcasses was a smelly, sweaty job. He spaded out a pit next to each carcass he discovered and poked the calf or cow into it with the shovel. The rain and sun had turned the flesh to jelly. He fought off swarms of horse flies while he struggled to get the chunks of rotted animals into the holes. Once he thought he heard a shot but he was deep in a gully and couldn't tell from which direction it came.

The sun was starting to slide toward Church Butte and he judged it must be nearly five o'clock when he called it quits and started back to headquarters. He was not tired and this pleased him. Except for the discouraging knowledge that marrying Nan was unlikely, he felt good.

When Handy rode into headquarters he found the men dressed for town but they hadn't left. They were shifting around uncomfortably. Jed and Jake were waiting for him.

"Thought maybe Nan would come in with you," Jed said. His voice sounded harsh. "You run across her?"

Jake was glowering fiercer than usual but he was silent.

"No." Handy was instantly alert and anxious. "Why?"

"She rode out after lunch," Jed said and there was worry in his eyes. "It's near suppertime and she's not come back. It's not like her. She's never gone more'n two, three hours."

"She took Little Sister?" Handy asked. He remembered the pony had stumbled when Nan had gone after the doc.

"It's her horse," Jed snapped. "She always rides her."

"She may have thrown Nan," Handy said. "She may be hurt."

"Or worse," Jed said bitterly, "with all the sheepmen and gunmen we got coming in." He turned and shouted to the crew, "Get a leg up. We're going out to look for Nan."

Handy stepped down, leaned the spade against the bunkhouse and went in. When he came out he was wearing his gun belt. He'd remembered the shot he'd heard while he was working in the gully.

Jed spread the men out in pairs covering an area from the river to the road. "Fire three shots, whoever finds her," he called.

Ron and Rod rode together and Roy went with Jed. The brothers were hard-faced and Handy thought they all looked accusingly at him. Jake rode with Handy. His eyes were fixed and expressionless, like an animal's when it is ready to make a kill. Handy, as tall and broad in the saddle, was grim and silent. They were a formidable pair. Handy thought he knew why Jake was riding with him. The range boss did not want Handy to be the one who found Nan.

"I know the trail Nan takes," Jake muttered and put the rowels to the buckskin's flanks. They were riding the high ground above the draws. "Let's get along. Nearing sundown."

Handy was so tense his chest ached. No one would harm Nan, he told himself, but the shot kept ringing in his ears and he remembered the three gamblers who had a score to settle with him. They might well have ridden onto the Lazy J looking for him and cut Nan's trail.

They galloped over the rolling land, up a hill and down a valley, past bunches of grazing cattle that neither moved nor raised their heads at the clop of the horses. There was a vastness to the endless hills that was chilling for its emptiness. Handy wondered why Nan chose to ride this lonely way.

"She liked to let her pony run," Jake muttered, as if he'd read the question when they trotted up another hill.

Handy remained silent. He did not care to share even his thoughts of Nan with Jake.

They topped another hill and across a mile of tableland Handy saw a distant figure walking down the trail. He kicked his horse into a gallop.

Jake had seen the person too. "There she is," he shouted and put the spurs to the buckskin. The tawny horse shook its mane and streaked off.

Handy's mustang could not match the buckskin's pace and he lagged behind. As they drew nearer, Handy saw that Nan was limping. Jake was off his horse and steadying her when Handy rode up. Nan's dusty cheeks were streaked with tears.

"What is it, what happened?" Jake was asking.

Nan sat on a flat rock and Jake hunkered beside her. Handy climbed down and went to her. "Are you hurt?" he asked.

She did not look at him but answered Jake. "Little Sister fell. She broke her leg and I had to shoot her."

"How'd you shoot her?" Jake looked puzzled. "You never carry a gun."

"I had this." Nan pulled the derringer from the waistband of her Levis and showed it to Jake. She jerked her head in Handy's direction. "He left it for me this morning." She glanced at Handy for the first time. Her eyes were hostile. "I don't want it. I don't want the kerchief, either."

Jake's eyes were cold when they turned on Handy. "I warned you, Southern. Stay away from Nan."

She did not contradict him.

Handy was confused and pained. He turned and fired three shots in the air. When he looked at Nan again her lips were thin and her eyes were bitter. He could not comprehend what had happened. He said, "Take my horse. It's not so far I can't walk."

"No need," Jake growled. "Nan can ride behind me." He lifted her to the buckskin's rump, and when he was in the saddle she put her arms around his waist.

Handy built a smoke and let them go on ahead.

◎◎◎◎◎◎◎◎◎◎◎◎◎

# CHAPTER XV

◎◎◎◎◎◎◎◎◎◎◎◎◎◎◎

Jed stormed into the cook shack while Handy was eating an early breakfast. He thought if he went to the target wheel, she might come down with some explanation of what was wrong when she heard him firing. Some of the men had returned during the night and others were drifting in now but he was the only one at the table.

"Damned sheep," Jed fumed. His mouth was grim and his eyes were cold. "Meant to ask last evening but got upset at Nan being gone. You see any sheep or herders yesterday?"

Li Shu brought Jed a cup of coffee. His smile faded and he hurried back to the kitchen when he saw Jed's face.

"Nope," Handy said. "Not a smell."

"How far you ride?"

"To the north range." Handy hadn't been off deeded land. "Get far onto it?"

"Just the edge." Handy finished his steak and cakes and Li Shu brought the coffeepot. "There was one deep draw where a dozen cows had been trapped. Took me a while."

"Damn!" Jed exclaimed and shook his grizzled head. "Well, we knew them cows was gone from the herd we put together. Thing now is the stinkers. Ed McCoy and Gene Garrison was here last evening. They got the X Bar and Slash Dot outfits north, other side of the river. They say we got sheep and herders both sides on the open range between us."

"I'm with the cattlemen," Handy said quietly. "I don't like sheep. But if the land is public domain, how you going to keep them off?"

"You know how," Jed said furiously. "They got no right

here. That land's cow country and it's ours. Always has been. We fought the Indians for it. Ain't just that. Sheep ruin it for cattle. Eat the grass down to the roots. Leave nothing but hard bare ground behind. Cows won't eat where sheep's been. Won't cross a sheep trail. Oil in the hooves of the stinkers smells up the ground so bad a cow can't stand it. Cows won't drink where sheep has watered. They'll drive us off if we allow them."

It sounded as if the war between the cattlemen and sheepmen were imminent. There'd be killing. Handy's sympathies were with the cattlemen but the sheepmen had a legal right to the open range. He was troubled. He said, "I guess it's coming then."

"It's damned near here," Jed said darkly. "Ed and Gene say a flock of three thousand head is trailing here from Oregon."

"Three thousand head!" It was a staggering figure.

The lines in Jed's face deepened. "They move that many head onto the range, our graze is gone. Never come back, not next year or the next. We're done. Can't let them get on the range." He finished his coffee and stood. "I want you to saddle up and take the trail west. They say the flock's somewhere in Idaho. I want to know where and how many and what's with them besides herders. When you find them come back fast as you can get here and tell me. Don't try to take them on by yourself alone." He stretched his lips in a tight smile. "Course, if you was to pick off two or three men from a distance, it'd be that many less we'd have to deal with. If they're coming here."

The prospect of several days, perhaps a week, in the saddle, alone on the trail, with a good horse under him and ample provisions should have pleased Handy, especially since he'd be away from Jake and the brothers. Instead it nagged him. He did not like the war clouds that were gathering on the horizon. He did not like Jed's assumption that he could bushwhack a man. Most of all, he did not like leaving the ranch for so long without the chance for a word with Nan, to discover what it was that had come between them. His heart was heavy at the way she'd treated him the evening before.

He kept looking toward the house while he saddled the mustang, tied on a blanket roll and canteen and filled the saddlebags. He wore his work clothes but took the hairpiece with him for safekeeping. With the Henry in the boot and the Walker Colt tied on his thigh, he swung into the saddle with a final backward look at the kitchen door. He thought someone was standing just inside but he could not be sure.

He did not ride into Green River but reined the mustang through the shallow stream and south and west toward Church Butte. Jed had told him that he'd cut the old Fremont Trail beyond Church Butte and that it was on this trail in Idaho that the flock had been reported. The land was arid and baked in the sun on the other side of the river and at a trot the mustang's hooves kicked up a plume of dust that feathered out behind. He wondered whether Nan was at her window watching and whether, if she still had Little Sister, she might have ridden out to overtake him. It was possible Nan's grief at having to shoot her pony had temporarily deranged her. She certainly had in no way been the normal Nan he'd known. He'd gone back for the saddle when Nan had gone to the ranch with Jake. The sight of the dead horse had pained him.

Abruptly he kicked the mustang into a gallop. Brooding over Nan would accomplish nothing, he told himself. He put her out of his mind.

When the sun was sinking, he made camp that day in some dry-leafed alders on Albert Creek beyond old Fort Bridger. There was enough water in the stream to fill the coffeepot. It had been a quiet day. He had passed only three ranches and met only two riders, cow pokes like himself. The pot was boiling on flat stones that edged the fire when at the sound of galloping hooves he dropped his hand to his gun. He remained squatted by the fire but waited, alert and ready, eyes traveling west along the trail.

A rider on a piebald was coming toward him, a small man in a broad-brimmed hat. He reined up beside the fire and sat in the saddle looking down at Handy with sharp brown eyes in a wizened monkey face. The man's hat was black, his vest and trousers were black and he wore a black string tie on a trail-dirtied white shirt. He was not armed.

"You're in a hurry, Parson," Handy said and grinned. "Got the devil on your tail?"

The preacher chuckled and said, "Smelled your coffee a mile off and couldn't get here soon enough."

"Take out your cup and hunker," Handy said and pointed to the boiling pot.

"Name's Luke," the preacher said and dropped to the ground. "Luke Ellsworth. And you're right. Traveling parson." He poured coffee into a tin cup from his saddlebag and squatted beside Handy.

"Southern, Handy Southern," Handy introduced himself. "Reckon you could do with some beans and sowbelly." He reached into the saddlebags he'd thrown to the ground when he'd unsaddled and hobbled the mustang.

"Thank you kindly, that I could," Parson Ellsworth said with enthusiasm. "Ain't et today."

"Oh?" Handy was surprised. "You off your circuit?"

"Quite a piece," the parson said ruefully. "Come from Idaho, halfway across the territory. Some kin of mine settled other side of Fort Bridger. Wrote me to come over and conduct services this morning and do some marrying and burying."

Handy sliced sowbelly with the Bowie knife and laid the slabs in a pan on the fire. "What held you up?"

"Sheep, dratted sheep, that was Friday," the preacher said disgustedly. "I was hardly two hours on the trail when I come up with this bunch of sheep. Couldn't get around them. Couldn't get through them. Biggest trail flock I ever seen. Took me near the entire day working my way through them. Them herders wasn't the Christian kind. They was making camp when I busted out all sweaty and panting for a drink of anything and didn't so much as ask me to share a drink of water."

"How many sheep would you say there were?" Handy asked quickly. He opened a can of beans with his knife.

"Thousands," the parson said and snorted. "Couldn't tell.

They was all around me. I was lost in them. Maybe five, ten thousand. The Good Book speaks kindly of the lamb but how them sheep do smell."

"It's taken you two days since to get this far," Handy said thoughtfully. It meant the flock still was a good day and a half's ride away. The sowbelly was sizzling and filling the air with its rich fragrance and the parson looked hungrily at it. Handy dumped the beans in the pan and laid four biscuits atop them.

"I rode fast," the preacher said. "Plumb tuckered Beelzebub." He laughed, a dry whisper in his throat. "Ain't blasphemous. Beelzebub's my horse."

Handy refilled their cups and scooped more water from the stream into the pot. He threw in another handful of Arbuckle's and put the pot back on the fire. "Turn out your horse to water and to feed, what grass there is. You can share my blanket."

"Thank you kindly," the parson said. "I'll water the horse and let him feed and I'll gladly share your supper but I'd best go on. Ain't so much farther and the folks will be worrying, what with the marrying and the burying set for tomorrow."

While they were sawing at the sowbelly and sopping up the sauce from the beans with the biscuits, Handy asked, "Were there others besides the herders with the sheep?"

"How you mean by that?" the preacher asked and reached for the coffeepot.

"Were there riders and were they armed?" Handy asked. "Were there wagons?"

"Oh, let's see." Parson Ellsworth frowned with the effort of concentration. "They was four, five, maybe six wagons, all covered. They was a good many men afoot and they was some riders, half a dozen, maybe more or less. Course they was armed. They's bears and other critters hereabouts like nothing better than to sink their teeth into a nice young lamb or even tough old ewe. They was carrying rifles and come to think on it, them riders was wearing sidearms like you."

Handy nodded his head gravely. The wagons meant a goodsized camp or several smaller camps. The riders meant armed guards. The herders were moving a large flock onto some range and they were equipped and prepared to stay. He asked, "Did you happen to overhear anything that indicated where they were headed with the sheep?"

"Couldn't hear a blessed thing with all that bleating in my ears." The preacher cackled. "Couldn't of heard Gabriel if he'd blowed his trumpet. Only thing I can tell you, they was headed this way."

After Preacher Ellsworth left, Handy thought he should have advised him to ride on to Green River. There might not be much marrying but there'd be burying aplenty in the valley. With the sheep outfits already reported on the range, this new flock with its armed guards was certain to provoke the shooting confrontation Jed had predicted. The days ahead loomed gray and grisly. Handy did not like killing but the coming rage on the range seemed inevitable.

He rode into the high country the next morning over rugged Bear Creek Divide with the trail squeezed through rocky passes where towering pine thrust skyward on either side. You could dynamite these passes and block the approaching flock, he thought, and dismissed the idea. The way would be cleared and there would be other sheep on the trail to the open grazing land. More and more, Jed's war seemed the only way to settle the hostility between the cattlemen and sheepmen. It would be a bloody fight to the finish.

He made early camp that night well off the trail on the Snake River Divide. The thin air was sharp and cold but when he'd eaten he doused his fire and slipped through the trees to a rock overhang above the trail. The flock was nearing Wyoming and he expected the flock boss would send outriders ahead to scout. The sheepmen would be aware of the feeling in the territory.

They came before sundown, two men of the faceless killer breed, cat-eyed and wary and armed with rifles and pistols. For several minutes they sat their bays on top of the divide and scoured the trail beyond. Finally, apparently satisfied no band of armed men was on the trail to this point, they returned the way they'd come at a bold, deliberate walk that was defiant and menacing. Handy remembered Jed's suggestion that he get some of the sheepmen in his sights if he had the chance. This was the opportunity but that was not his way.

He rolled up in his blanket at dusk and was on the trail at dawn, searching for some vantage point where he could observe the flock and not be trapped behind it. A wooded elevation overlooking a broad mountain meadow with a small stream running through the grass seemed a likely spot. The place, in fact, amused him. Coming off the trail into such a pasture, the flock would spread out and graze and the herders would find the sheep uncontrollable. He tethered the mustang in the trees off the trail and stretched out on a mound to wait. The Henry rifle was by his side.

The sun warmed the air and the hours dragged on. To keep from thinking of Nan, he turned Jake over in his mind and inspected him. He could find nothing in Jake's make-up to change his opinion that Jake was the orneriest critter he'd ever come across. There was no doubt the man had saved his life but there was a limit to which a man could go to repay even such a heavy obligation. Handy himself would try not to provoke the situation but the time would come when Jake and he would settle their differences with their fists. His reaction when he thought Jake had stolen the hairpiece was evidence of that.

The sun was nearly overhead when two outriders came out of the trees on the trail across the wide meadow. When they reached the stream, they dismounted and let their bays drink. Handy was certain they were the same riders he'd seen the night before. A good half hour passed before a faint bleating reached his ears and sheep spilled into the meadow, hundreds of them, thousands of them. Handy kept a quick count as they came from the trees into the pasture. His final estimate as the last of the rams, ewes and lambs spread across the meadow staggered him. He put the flock at five thousand head.

Accompanying the sheep were fifteen armed guards, two dozen herders on foot and six covered wagons.

With the appearance of the first sheep, the two outriders

had swung into their saddles and started across the meadow. Although he felt trapped, Handy had not moved, but the riders had dismounted again at the foot of the mound where he lay. Now he slithered back into the trees and led the mustang to the trail. When he was in the saddle, he kicked its flanks and galloped off. He'd ridden a good half mile when a shot sang behind him. He could tell by the sound that it was out of range and he did not turn with his Henry to return the fire. The first shot of the war had been fired by the sheepmen.

◎◎◎◎◎◎◎◎◎◎◎◎◎◎

# CHAPTER XVI

◎◎◎◎◎◎◎◎◎◎◎◎◎◎

Jed's seamed face went gray under the leathery skin when Handy reported what he'd seen to him in his office.

"We got to stop them," he shouted furiously. "I'll round up all the ranchers and their men. We'll band together, muster up a army and go out to fight them."

"We'd be dead wrong," Handy said quietly. "We don't know they're coming here. Even if they do, we have no legal right to drive them off unless they trespass deeded land."

"Law be damned," Jed roared. "We got a right to protect what's ours."

"If we go out and attack them, they'll have right on their side," Handy pointed out. "The cattlemen will have an army of U.S. marshals or maybe the Army of the United States rounding them up to stand trial. We've got to do something but there must be another way."

"What other way is there they'd understand excepting guns?" Jed demanded. He fell silent and sat staring at the gun cabinet. His eyes began to gleam craftily. At last he said, "Maybe you're right. I think I know what you mean. Guns, but not in the open. More like vigilante raiding parties in the night. I should of known you'd have the answer."

Vigilante raids were not the answer but Handy made no comment. At the moment he had no solution to the problem.

"Yes, sir, you hit on it," Jed said approvingly. "I'll tell you what I want you to do. There's a sheep camp off the far edge of the north range. Ride up there tonight and shoot two or three herders. Give the sheepmen warning of what's coming if they don't stay off."

The order stunned Handy. He said, "I'd do almost anything for you, Jed, but I can't do that."

"What the hell kind of talk is that for a gunman?" Jed asked angrily.

"Is that what you thought I was, a hired gun?" Handy asked slowly. He felt as if his horse had tromped the wind from him.

"Ain't you?" Jed said roughly. "The way you wear your gun, the way you shoot, the things you said. Don't worry. If it's money I'll pay you better'n you been paid before."

Handy felt numb. Now he fully understood Jed's many oblique remarks and considerations. He could only repeat, "I am not a gunman."

"If you ain't a gunslinger, what are you?" Jed asked scornfully.

"Sorry, Jed, if I gave you cause to read sign wrong," Handy said hollowly. "I was a cattleman, like yourself, only much smaller, with my sister, before the Indians killed her and burned us out. I've been drifting since, working as a hand. My Pa was a pilgrim, came out here from Ohio and took up ranching. He never wore a gun and never learned to shoot. Folks looked down on him for that, and when I was a small boy I decided I was going to be the best shot in the territory. I've been handling guns since I could walk because my Pa couldn't. I've killed when I've been called and I'd do it again but I can't shoot a man in cold blood."

Jed stared at him without speaking.

"I guess that's why you kept me, because you thought this battle with the sheepmen was coming and I'd be useful," Handy went on. "I'll stay and work without salary until you consider I've paid for the doctor and my care and then I'll drift."

Jed's face gradually softened and he said, almost gently, "I like you, son, have from the beginning. I guess I'm glad you're not a gunman. You're a man I can admire. Far as drifting is concerned, don't give that notion no heed. You earn your found and salary and more to boot. There's a place for you—I want you here." Abruptly, he laughed heartily. "The joke's on Jake. Was him said you was a gunslinger."

What Jed had said put warm blood in Handy. He said, "Thank you, Jed. I don't want to leave. I'm a good hand and I'll earn my keep. If you like, I'll ride up to the sheep camp and warn them to keep off the north range."

Jed considered and his face went hard again. "It might be a good idea. Find out what you can. Even if you ain't a gunman, you're in for a fight. We can't let the sheepmen drive us off our range."

"Anybody shoots in my direction, I'll return the fire, but there must be another way," Handy said. "I'll ride up after I've eaten."

He looked hopefully for Nan when he left the office but only Full Moon was in the kitchen and Nan was not in the yard.

Roy clomped from the cook shack as Handy approached the stoop. "I want a word with you, Handy," he said and stomped to the side of the building.

Handy followed irritably. He was in no mood to be badgered. "What's it now?" he asked shortly.

"Just wanted you to know," Roy said deliberately as if the words came hard, "we didn't rightly see what you done for us when we was in town last week. We was that drunk. At Trail's End Ralph told us how you stood up for us and got our money back and Little Red told us how you brung us to the ranch tied to the saddles when we couldn't ride. We'd take it kindly if you didn't think too bad of us, the way we been going out of our way to make life miserable for you. Won't be no more things like that."

"Forget it," Handy said and grinned. He was pleased Roy had made the effort, which must have cost him sorely.

Roy offered his hand. "Shake?"

"Sure."

Roy gripped Handy's palm and departed solemnly.

Handy looked for a glimpse of Nan after he'd eaten—but did not see her. He hoped she hadn't left the ranch again. He'd reported directly to Jed as soon as he'd returned and had left the mustang in the corral saddled. There still was food in the bags and the blanket roll still was at the cantle. He thought he'd make camp and ride back early in the morning. He felt he should try to sort things out.

The day was warm and the mustang had been ridden hard so Handy let it walk, only occasionally lifting it to a trot. He took the trail Nan usually rode, not that he had much hope of seeing her but because it was the most direct route to the north range. Cattle looking sleekly beefed out grazed on the browning grass and now and then he saw a hand in the distance. At the place where Nan's pony had fallen there was recently spaded ground and the thought flashed across his mind that Jake had buried the horse and Nan had ridden out with him. The picture of Nan riding back to the ranch behind Jake with her arms around him put Handy in a gloomy state of mind and when he saw the range boss coming down the trail he looked hard at him but did not rein in his mount.

Jake pulled his buckskin up nose to nose with the mustang and it was a stand-off. "You're back," Jake grunted. "What you find?"

Handy glared at Jake a moment before answering and the big flat-eyed man scowled. Handy said tonelessly, "There's a big flock on the trail, about five thousand head, with herders and wagons and fifteen armed guards."

"They coming here?" Jake barked.

"I didn't ask them," Handy snapped back. "They're headed in this direction."

"If they come here you got your work laid out for you, gunslinger," Jake said. "We all have."

Handy said nothing but he felt his gut tighten.

"How come you to be walking your horse?" Jake asked.

"The horse is weary," Handy told him.

"What you doing out here?" Jake asked belligerently. "Looking for Nan?"

"Jed sent me to the sheep camp," Handy said evenly.

Jake's beard lifted and fell as he chewed the inside of his cheek. "So lever your Henry and start to earn your keep," he muttered and roweled the buckskin's flanks.

Jed had said a length of bob wire separated the north range from the open range. The fence was not to keep the cattle on one side or the other but only to indicate to hands with cows on the open range the beginning of the deeded land.

"You'll see it off maybe half a mile when you come up out of a valley," Jed had said.

The valley was a cup and the hill beyond was steep. The mustang dug in and pawed its way to the top. As Handy's eyes came into view of the tableland a rifle shot rang over his head. He rolled from the saddle with the Henry in his fist and spanked the mustang down into the valley. In the brief glimpse he'd had of the graze ahead, he'd seen sheep and they were on Jed's deeded land.

He pulled off his hat and, when he'd bellied near the top, edged it on the rifle barrel above the lip of the tableland. A bullet zinged through the crown from straight ahead. He dropped the hat, moved well to the left and lifted quickly to snap a shot at a rider on a roan facing the valley. The man dropped his rifle and keeled over the neck of his horse. Beyond a flock of about two hundred sheep the herder was running away. A sheepdog remained with the sheep, which grazed placidly. As Handy looked back to the man he'd shot, the rider toppled to the ground with one boot still in a stirrup.

Handy ran down to the mustang and rode up to the high flat pasture. He pulled the guard's boot from the stirrup and turned the man over to see where he'd shot him. The gunman was the weasel-faced gambler from the saloon whose derringer he'd taken. His shot had been a bad one. The bullet had creased the skull. The gunman was unconscious but he was not dead. Handy pulled off the gun belt and pistol and strapped it on, crisscrossing his own belt. He hogtied the man, mounted and took off at a gallop after the fleeing herder. He overtook him before he reached the fence.

The herder was a Mexican, a ragged, brown-faced little man with terror in his dark eyes. He fell to his knees and lifted clasped hands.

"*Por dios,*" he implored.

"*¿Habla inglés?*" Handy asked.

"*No. Por dios, señor, por dios.*" The herder was crying.

Handy said in Spanish, "It is not right that you feed the sheep where you do. This is the land of the don Maine. He is very angry that you place sheep on cow grass. It would please him if I would kill you and shoot the sheep. I shall not do this because I want you to do a thing for me. Gather them and drive them where the others are. I know there must be two more camps where men like the one I shot are guarding the flocks. Tell them I have killed their friend and will do the same for them when I find them. They would be wise to remove the sheep entirely from this land."

"*Si, señor. Gracias, mil gracias.*" The herder turned and ran toward the flock.

Handy saw the sheep wagon standing not far beyond Jed's fence. It had been no accident the flock was grazing on his land. He went back to the gunman. He was conscious and spat viciously at him.

"Better mind your manners," Handy said quietly. "My orders were to kill anyone this side of the fence. I'm going to take you in alive. I'll untie your feet and help you into the saddle but I'll shoot you if you make one false move."

When the rope was off the boots, he boosted the gunman into the saddle, picked up his rifle and climbed onto the mustang with the end of the rope tied around the pommel.

"When we're out of the valley, kick your horse into a steady trot," he called. With the captive on his hands, he wanted to return to headquarters before dark.

The gunman didn't speak during the entire ride. Handy kept thinking of the other two. He was certain there were at least two other sheep camps. He thought it likely that these outfits had been sent onto the range ahead of the big flock to test the ranchers.

It was dusk when he reached headquarters with his prisoner. Some of the hands were at the corral building smokes after supper and they hopped down to peer curiously at the gunman and at Handy with his two gun belts and two rifles.

"What'd he do?" Little Red sang out when Handy steadied the gunman out of the saddle and hogtied him on the ground.

"Shot at me," Handy grunted and carried his rifle into the bunkhouse. When he came out Little Red was prodding the gunman with the toe of his boot. "Leave him be," Handy told him. "If you want to be useful, unsaddle the horses and turn them out."

He did not see Jake, either at the corral or when he walked to the house carrying the gunman's Winchester.

Nan came to the kitchen door when he knocked. Her eyes chilled when she saw him and dropped to the two gun belts and the rifle.

"Nan," he said urgently. "I've got to talk with you but I can't right now. It's important that we talk. May I see you later?"

"Pa's in his office," she answered and walked away.

Jake was with Jed, sitting in a chair in front of the desk. He lifted a corner of his lip over his dog tooth when he saw the crossed gun belts. "A two-gunslinger," he jeered. "Get yourself a scalp?"

"Close your mouth, Jake," Jed snapped. His eyes were hard when he looked at Handy. "What'd you come up with?"

"Sheep, our side of the fence," Handy said. He unstrapped the gun belt and laid it with the Army Colt in the holster on Jed's desk. The rifle he leaned against the gun cabinet. "An armed guard and one herder."

"You killed them both," Jake assumed. "And the sheep?"

"I nicked the guard and brought him back alive," Handy said calmly.

"What the hell," Jake said angrily. "You're hired to kill, not take prisoners."

Apparently Jed had not informed Jake that Handy was not a gunslinger. Handy did not enlighten him.

"What did you do about the herder and the sheep?" Jed asked.

"Threw a scare in him and he drove the sheep off," Handy

said. "They'll not be near your graze again. The herder thinks I killed the guard."

"Damn it, you should of killed the herder and them sheep," Jed said bitterly. "They ruined that end of my graze. How come you to only wound the guard and bring him in alive?"

"It was a jump shot," Handy said. "He had me pinned down in the valley and I grazed him. Reason I brought him in is I know two other gunmen are on the range and probably with flocks. Saw them with this one at Trail's End. I thought he could tell us where the camps are and whether they have anything to do with that big flock that's moving this way, before we turn him over to the marshal."

"Hell with the marshal," Jake snarled. "We'll string him up when he's talked."

"Shut your mouth," Jed told him and asked, "Where is he now?"

"Hogtied," Handy said. "Out by the corral."

"Let's go talk to him," Jed said and left the desk.

Jake looked at Handy and sneered, "Yellow-livered gunslinger." He followed Jed.

Handy did not see Nan when he went out through the kitchen.

All the hands who were at headquarters were gathered about the bound man on the ground and even Li Shu had stepped onto the cook-shack stoop to watch.

"Untie his feet and get him up," Jed told Handy. With the glowering gunman facing him, Jed said harshly, "The orders was to kill anybody found on my land. You want to stay breathing, you answer my questions. How many sheep outfits is moved onto the range?"

The gunman glared at Jed and did not answer.

"I'll ask once more," Jed said. "You talk or I'll tell the boys to string you up."

The man kept his teeth clamped.

Jed turned on his heel. "Put him to the rope," he told Jake and started toward the house.

"Wait," the prisoner called.

Jed turned. "Well?"

"What you aim to do with me if I talk?" the gunman asked.

"Turn you over to the marshal," Jed said brusquely. "You was running stinkers on deeded land. You tried to kill my man."

"What was it you wanted to know?" the prisoner asked.

"How many sheep camps and where are they?" Jed repeated.

"They's two others," the man muttered. "They's way back in."

"Armed guards with them like you was?" Jed asked.

"Guess so."

"Same sized flocks?" Jed asked.

"Guess so, 'bout two hundred head in each." The man was sullen. "We got as much right to open range as you."

"Not by a damn sight you ain't," Jed said explosively. "This is cow country. You was off the range anyhow. Looks sort of expensive, putting a armed guard on two hundred head. You expecting company?"

The man did not answer.

"We know they's five thousand head of sheep on the trail and a army of gunmen with them," Jed said. "They coming here?"

"Sure they're coming here, to the open range," the man said defiantly. "You best leave them be or they'll have your hides."

"All this one outfit?" Jed asked. "The three camps on the range and this big flock? Who's behind it?"

"Man named Smathers," the gunman said. "He ain't come yet but he will and he'll be ready for you."

Jed glanced at Handy. "You done right to bring him in," he said and turned to Jake. "Take him to the marshal. Tell him what he done."

"I'll take him in," Handy said quickly.

"You ain't et," Jed told him, considerately. "You already put in a full day. Go to the cook shack and tell Li Shu to fry you up a big steak."

Handy was troubled and disturbed while he ate supper that Jake was taking the prisoner to jail. He thought the big man with the blue-green eyes that showed no depth was not only mean but bloodthirsty. He was deeply concerned when Big Jake stomped into the cook shack before he'd finished his supper, poured a cup of coffee and sat across the table from him.

"What happened?" Handy asked tightly.

There was a curious gleam in Jake's eyes, like the glow from a gem stone, when he said, "Man tried to escape in the dark. Had to shoot him. Finished off the job you was hired to do."

# CHAPTER XVII

◎◎◎◎◎◎◎◎◎◎◎◎◎◎

After supper the next evening, Handy left his gun belt in the bunkhouse and took the Henry rifle down to the target wheel. He was considerably annoyed at his near miss when he'd snapped off the jump shot at the gunman. He'd been lucky. His life had depended on that shot. The aces on the wheel had long since been shredded and he was working his way through the other cards in the four old decks Jed had given him. This night he tacked up nines.

It was September. The feel of autumn was in the air and dusk came earlier. He now had a scant hour of light to shoot. When he had the cards on the spokes, he gave the wheel a spin, paced off five hundred yards, hunkered with his back to the target, sprang to his feet, whirled and fired. He quickly levered another and went to examine the cards. He'd missed the long middle pip on both although one shot was only a hair above it.

He'd fired half a dozen rounds from the squat and was at the wheel again when he heard someone walking toward him. His heart sent blood surging through his veins and he turned to greet Nan. It was Jed.

The old rancher put more wrinkles in his face with a smile and asked, "Hard put to bear your shot at the gunman?"

Handy's eyes slitted and he shook his head. "Hard put to bear Jake's gunning him down."

"He was running off," Jed said defensively.

"You don't believe that any more than I do," Handy contradicted. "If I'd killed him in a gunfight when he'd put his sights on me, it would have been a different matter. Or if you'd strung him up for firing at me and running sheep on your land. But you agreed to turn him over to the marshal if he talked. Jake plain murdered him."

"It ain't no great loss, but reckon you're right," Jed said and scowled. "A man's word is his bond whoever he gives it to and Jake ain't trustworthy. Maybe he did it for the horse and saddle."

"I doubt it," Handy said. "He could have taken them anyway. I saw the roan in the horse pasture this morning. It's a fine horse."

"That horse and saddle is rightly yours," Jed said. "And the Winchester and Colt you left in the office."

"I was on salary, on business and on your property," Handy pointed out. "They belong to you. If you want, consider the guns a trade for the ones you gave me. Jake killed a man and stole his horse. That's different."

"Maybe there's some sense in your thinking, but I ain't certain," Jed said doubtfully. "How some ever, Jake ain't what I come down here for. I want you to ride out tomorrow morning and see how far the sheep is come."

"Sure," Handy agreed at once. He'd be happy to be away from Jake for the day.

Although Handy was up before dawn, Li Shu showed a light in the cook shack and he went in for coffee and whatever the Chinaman had ready.

"What long, you, Missy Nan?" Li Shu singsonged as he fried eggs and potatoes.

The warmth from the range had been inviting on this chilly morning and Handy was in the kitchen. He took a slow swallow of coffee before answering. "Damned if I know. She won't talk to me."

"Full Moon say Missy Nan not happy again and don' eat." The cook's almond-shaped eyes peered intently at Handy. "You say, do something she don' like?"

"I must have," Handy said, "but I can't find out what because she won't stand still and let me ask her."

"Maybe somebody tell she some thing ain't so 'bout you," Li Shu suggested.

Handy filled his canteen with coffee and took jerky and a handful of biscuits when he'd finished eating to take along for lunch.

The night was draining from the sky when he went to the horse pasture for the mustang. The roan snorted and tossed its long black mane when it saw him. He went to it and rubbed its nose. The red horse had a fine head and stood a good sixteen hands. It was an animal a man could admire. Perhaps Jake actually had shot the gunman for the horse, although Handy preferred to think he'd murdered him because the range boss was cruel and liked to kill.

He rode crosscountry again in the pale blue early day but followed closer to the river to cut the trail well this side of Church Butte. He did not think the sheep could have moved as far as Fort Bridger in the two days since he'd seen them in the mountain meadow, but he was wary of the outriders and did not want them behind him.

Li Shu's curious observation that someone may have degraded him to Nan disturbed him. It was possible that Jake, or the brothers before they made their peace with him, had warned her against him, but what could they have said that had made such a difference? She acted as if she resented him. He felt helpless. You couldn't strike something down when you didn't know what you were fighting.

It was noon and he was several miles beyond Fort Bridger when he sighted the flock in the distance and pulled the mustang up. The sheep were not on the trail. They were spread out on either side grazing on the sparse dry grass. He saw no outriders and the herders appeared to be holding the flock. He watched for perhaps half an hour and still the herders made no move to gather the sheep and start them off. After he'd munched biscuits and jerky and washed them down with cold coffee, he pulled the mustang around and started back. Was it possible one of the other gunmen had ridden out with word the cattlemen were taking up arms against the sheep camps?

The night sky was dark and it was turning cold when he reached the Lazy J. He unsaddled the mustang and put him to pasture and left his saddlebags and guns in the bunkhouse before he went to Jed's back door. A lamp was burning in the kitchen. He thought he'd find Jed at the table with a cup of coffee. Nan came to the door when he knocked.

"Nan, what is wrong, what have I done?" he implored.

Tears welled in her eyes and her lips trembled. He thought she was going to relent but she bit her lip and said, "Pa's not here."

"Please, may I come in and talk with you?" he asked gently.

"No," she cried. A sob escaped before she closed the door.

He asked Li Shu whether he knew where Jed was when he went to the cook shack. It was past suppertime and they were alone.

"Mista Jed go by Jake and Lon and Loy and Lod," the friendly small cook told him and ladled stew on his dish.

The smell filled Handy's throat. "This sheep?" he asked.

"Oh, yes," Li Shu said and smiled. "Velly good kind son-of-a-bitch."

"You have any pie?"

"Fo' you, laisin pie," Li Shu confided. "You like?"

"Yes." Handy pushed the mutton stew to one side. "I'm not hungry. Just the pie and coffee."

It was Friday and not strange that Jake and the brothers should go to Green River but it was beyond belief that Jed would accompany them.

Although Handy had spent the day in the saddle, sleep wouldn't come to him that night and he still was awake when the brothers came into the bunkhouse. It must have been midnight. They were not noisy as they usually were and they did not seem to be drunk. A few minutes later Jake clomped in and then he heard the back door at the house bang shut. The five of them made an unlikely group and he lay awake for at least another hour pondering what possible common interest could have drawn them together. He finally drowsed off but his sleep was uneasy.

Before going to the cook shack in the morning, he knocked at the back door of the white house again and it was Jed's voice that called to come in. He was at the table and his breakfast plate was before him. Full Moon was poking wood into the range and did not look about.

"Well?" Jed said gruffly. His face looked drawn and his shoulders seemed to sag.

"The flock is on the other side of Fort Bridger but the sheep aren't moving," Handy told Jed. He seemed to be only half listening and he stared at his stack of cakes without putting his fork to them. Handy went on, "They seem to be holding the sheep there. I can't understand why unless they're not certain of their plans."

"I hope to hell they don't come here," Jed muttered. "Don't know where or how it's going to end."

"There must be land enough for everyone in the territory," Handy said.

"You saw how it was this year," Jed grumbled. "Nothing for the cows to eat. There ain't all that much good grassland."

Jake was in the cook shack wolfing a steak and a pile of fried potatoes when Handy went in for breakfast. "There's a bunch of cows that's strayed downstream off the Lazy J," he said to Handy. "Get them back on home range." He looked craftily at him and unexpectedly laughed gustily. "Afore some sheepmen come across them and slices them up for beefsteaks just for spite."

The brothers had not come in for breakfast but whatever they'd all been doing the night before seemed to agree with Jake.

The cattle had wandered almost all the way to Green River and Handy enjoyed the ride in the sun and being away from headquarters. Jake was a constant irritant and Nan disturbed him deeply. Jed had appeared troubled that morning and that was another worry.

There were half a dozen cantankerous cows that didn't want to go back home and it was late afternoon by the time Handy had driven them onto the north range. It was Saturday and the hands were togging out for town. Handy still had almost four dollars from the advance Jed had given him and was dispirited. He scrubbed, changed clothes and put on his gun belt and hairpiece. He'd decided a few belts of whiskey would help him sleep.

Before going to the murky Trail's End, where there was sure to be a hubbub, he tied up at Doc Bainbridge's. He was reluctant to ask the doc the favor he had in mind but he was desperate.

"It's Nan," he said, sitting beside the desk-operating table. "I can't make her out. Right from the beginning she was friendly and sociable. Lately she's not even civil, won't pass the time of day. She acts like I've done something that has hurt her. If I have I'm damned if I know what it can be."

The doc pushed his spectacles up on his nose and lifted his eyebrows. "She seemed to hold you in high regard," he said. "She's a reasonable young lady. Why don't you talk with her?"

"I've tried to, several times," Handy said despairingly. "She refuses to have a word with me."

"I don't know how I can help," the doc said regretfully. "I don't know what to say because I don't know the circumstances."

"That's it," Handy said hopefully. "If you knew what was in her mind, maybe you could advise me. She respects you and would talk with you. I thought if you could drop in like you were just passing by and have a chat with her, something might come of it." He fished three cartwheels from his pocket and laid them on the desk. "It isn't much, I know, to pay for such a call, but I'll make it up when I'm paid."

The doc's eyes twinkled and he laughed. He pushed the coins back to Handy. "If I'm to be the intermediary in an affair of the heart, it has to be as a friend and not a doctor."

Handy felt his cheeks flush.

The doc chuckled and went on, "Sure, Handy. I'll drive by but I won't charge a fee for it." He laughed again. "I've a prescription right now for what ails you. Take some whiskey."

"I was aiming to do just that," Handy said and grinned.

Green River's dirt Main Street was jam-packed with riders and men afoot but it was early and the boys had not started any trouble. Empty wagons waited in front of stores with false fronts where lamps dimly lighted staples and merchandise and the hitch rails in front of the saloons were lined. A full-throated challenge to the night roared over each pair of bat-wings. Handy found room for the mustang at Trail's End and a place for his elbow on the bar. He did not see anyone from the Lazy J in the bawling crowd of pokes from the half-dozen ranches in the valley. He understood Jed's men usually started at the first saloon at the north end of Main Street and worked their way down to the Trail's End.

Handy was working on his second glass of whiskey when the batwings flew apart and a tousled waddy burst in. His face was red with excitement and his eyes were blazing. He bellied up to the bar and demanded whiskey. "They got what was coming to them," he shouted at Ralph, the bull-necked bartender, in a voice loud enough for all to hear above the commotion. "They give them hell at them three camps."

"Chew it finer," Ralph said as the uproar faded and the men at the bar turned to stare at the poke.

Now that he had the attention of the house, the newcomer sipped his whiskey leisurely. Finally he said, "Was coming across the open range from the Slash Dot. There is, or *was*, three sheep outfits there." He paused. "Ain't no more."

"Go on," Ralph said impatiently when the hand stopped talking. "They move out?"

"Nope," the cowboy said and smiled with satisfaction. "Wagons is burned out. Most sheep is dead, clubbed and shot. What ewes is still alive is crying over dead lambs. Two herders is dead. Two what looked like guards shot through the head. Damndest slaughter I ever see. That'll teach them sheepmen."

Suddenly the whiskey lay sour on Handy's stomach. He shoved from the bar and stalked out. He knew where Jed and Jake and the brothers had been the night before.

◎◎◎◎◎◎◎◎◎◎◎◎◎◎

# CHAPTER XVIII

◎◎◎◎◎◎◎◎◎◎◎◎◎◎

When the work load permitted, Jed gave half the crew Sundays off, alternating from week to week. Handy was free this day. He breakfasted at dawn's first faint light to avoid the others and saddled the mustang. On the trail to the north range, he kicked the horse into a hard gallop. He did not wear his gun belt.

The carnage he'd heard described at the saloon the night before physically sickened him. Wanton killing of humans and animals was no solution to the differences between the cattlemen and sheepmen. There had to be some middle ground where they could reach a compromise. He had no ready answer and he did not know what he would do. He did not see how he could stay on at the Lazy J and participate in the impending warfare as he'd be required.

At the bob-wire fence that marked the edge of Jed's deeded land, he hesitated only briefly and rode around it onto the open range. The sheep and wagon had been moved. Circling black turkey buzzards in the sky some miles off directed him to the remains. The scorched land about an embered wagon was littered with the blood-drenched carcasses of two hundred ewes and lambs on which the obscene birds were feeding. He searched, scattering the dark, protesting scavengers, but found no bodies here. He did not go on. The nauseating stench and sight drove him off the open range.

It was not yet lunchtime and when he'd turned the mustang out he climbed onto the top rail of the corral and was building a smoke when he saw a rider coming down the road to headquarters. He looked spare and rangy and rode tall in his saddle.

As he neared, Handy saw he had a craggy face and granite-gray eyes. He wore the star of a United States marshal on his vest.

The marshal ground-reined his horse and knocked at the front door. Jed stepped onto the porch and Handy heard the marshal say, "I've come for Southern."

Handy jumped down and walked toward the house. Jed saw him coming and said nothing. The marshal swung about, saw him and waited.

"I'm Southern," Handy said calmly. "What do you want with me?"

"You're charged with murder," the marshal said in a gravelly voice and unhooked hand irons from his belt.

"Just a minute, Bob," Jed objected angrily.

"Whose murder?" Handy demanded.

"Five counts of murder and slaughtering six hundred head of sheep on public domain." He confronted Handy dangling the cuffs. "Put out your hands."

Handy thought he heard a gasp from inside the house.

"Hold on," Jed thundered.

"I heard of it," Handy said, "last night at Trail's End. I rode out myself this morning to see whether it was true. It was. I had no part in it."

"You can tell that to the jury," Bob, the marshal, said coldly. He reached for Handy's wrist with an open iron.

"Damn it, Bob, I told you to hold up," Jed exploded. "When this supposed to of took place?"

"Friday night," Bob said irritably and shook the cuffs.

"What time?" Jed barked.

"A good spell after dark, about ten I guess," the marshal snapped impatiently. "What's that got to do with it?"

"Use your head," Jed growled, calmer now. "First place, how could one man of killed five and done in six hundred sheep?"

"There were others," the marshal said harshly. "A drove of them. Southern was identified by a herder that escaped."

"Second place," Jed declared, "how could he of been identified when he was here at headquarters all of Friday evening? I can vouch for that."

Nan ran onto the porch. She was crying. "I can too," she sobbed. "He came to the door just after supper. Li Shu can tell you too. He went to the bunkhouse after the cook shack and didn't come out again. I know. I was watching from the kitchen."

Handy felt a gladness spread through him at her words and her defense.

The marshal put a perplexed frown under his fawn-colored John B. "Maybe so, if you folks back him up like you do. Maybe he didn't ride in the raids on the camps Friday night but he killed a man that was guarding the sheep the day before. It was witnessed. That herder that escaped the massacre. He walked to town. Got in this morning. He's a greaser. Had a time of it finding somebody who spoke his lingo but I finally got it out of him. He described the man he saw kill a sheep guard Thursday off the north end of your range. Went to Trail's End and talked to Ralph. That man was Southern."

"The gunman and herder and sheep were trespassing on my deeded land." Jed wiped his mouth and flung defiance at the marshal. "Don't believe they was on my graze, I'll take you up there and you can smell the ground. Southern come up with them on my land and the gunman put down on Southern. He had every right and should of killed the gunslinger but he didn't. He took him prisoner and brought him in alive. All the hands was here and seen it and will tell you that."

The marshal seemed perplexed. "What happened to him?"

Jake had walked up unnoticed. "I shot him," he growled before Jed could answer. "I was bringing him in to you and he tried to get away. He was a prisoner who'd broke the law and he was trying to escape."

The marshal thumbed back his Stetson and let out his breath. "Where's the body?"

"Somewheres half a mile down and off the road where he'd took off when I stopped him with my gun." Jake looked balefully at the marshal. "You see any wrong in what I done?"

"Not the way you tell it," the marshal said skeptically. "Got to take your word that's the way it happened and Jed says the man was on his land. Nobody to say otherwise." He swung back to Handy and tucked the hand irons back in his belt. "Nothing 'gainst you, Southern, least that can stand up. There seem to be good people siding you." To Jed he said, "Anything you know about the killings on the range?"

"My men's all accounted for," Jed said stoutly. "I back them. They hadn't had nothing to do with it."

The way Jed was putting on made the bile gorge up in Handy and he turned his back.

"Shame, this killing," the marshal said. "Not much I can do now. The herder that got away was too scared to see anything like brands and the riders were all masked. I'll be getting on."

"Come in for coffee and some pie," Jed invited.

Handy wanted to get away again. Jed's act was too much for him.

"Thanks kindly but I'd better not," Bob said. "I'll have to find that body and bring it in."

"I'll show you where," Jake offered. "Soon's I saddle up."

The marshal went with him and Jed slumped into the house. Nan remained on the porch. She looked at him and there was sadness in her.

Handy smiled tentatively and said, "Thank you, Nan, for speaking for me as you did."

"It doesn't change things," she said and sounded wretched. "It's that I knew you had no hand in it this time." She went back into the house before he could say more.

He stepped from the porch and walked around the house. The marshal waited for Jake outside the barn. Handy wondered whether Jake would have admitted killing the gunman if Jed hadn't been there. It had been outright murder and he thought the marshal knew it.

He was on his way to the cook shack when Jed called him from the back door. "Want a word, son."

Handy had no inclination for words with Jed but he went to the kitchen and followed him into his office.

"Sit down," Jed said, and when he was at his desk, "Think we done it, don't you?"

"The idea's been gnawing at my mind," Handy admitted bitterly. "Didn't you?"

"No," Jed said weightily as if the denial were an effort. "Least not me. I was at the X Bar talking with Ed McCoy and Gene Garrison about what to do. Rode off the same time Jake and the boys lit out, come back right after them. They was supposed to see Norm Ring on up the river. Can't say they had a hand in those attacks, can't say they didn't and ain't going to ask."

"Thanks, Jed," Handy said quietly. He believed Jed. "The way things stand we'll never know and it's better not to voice suspicions that can't be backed up. What did you and your friends decide to do?"

"Reckon we got no choice," Jed said heavily. "Five, six thousand head of sheep is a mighty big flock. We figure to meet them head-on afore they reach the range. We'll talk peaceable if they'll listen to reason. If they won't we'll have to convince them with our guns."

"I guess there's no other way," Handy said. "When is the showdown?"

"It's like you been telling me, we got to wait until they show their clear intention they're making for our range," Jed said. "Otherwise they could say they wasn't heading here and if there's killing that we provoked them. Only way for them to get to the open range without crossing deeded land is through Green River and on the road past here. They'll have to show their hand in five, six days."

Handy nodded his head. "All right, Jed, the way you put it now I can live with it. I'll be siding you if we have to fight."

◎◎◎◎◎◎◎◎◎◎◎◎◎◎

# CHAPTER XIX

◎◎◎◎◎◎◎◎◎◎◎◎◎◎

Nan was on the porch rocking in her Pa's chair and trying to get Handy out of her mind when she saw Dr. Bainbridge's buggy coming down the road on this bright Sunday afternoon. She was surprised and pleased, happy she hadn't taken Juliet, Little Sister's dam, for the ride that she'd considered. The doctor stopped, waved and climbed down as if his bones were creaky.

"Pa's out," she said, "but come in for coffee and there's an apple pie."

"Don't know as I'm sorry Jed's not here," the doctor said and brightened his face with a smile. "More enjoyable to chat with a lovely young lady. Wasn't anything important, anyway. Never see Jed in town. Was nearby and thought to say hello."

"Such gallantry," she said and laughed and led him to the kitchen. "And such a fibber. Sit down at the table. The pot is on the stove. I'll pour a cup and cut the pie."

"Where's Jed off to on Sunday?" the doctor asked and pulled out a chair at the big table covered with a blue and white checkerboard cloth.

"There have been killings on the public land, men and sheep," she said gravely. "Pa went up to see for himself."

"I heard something about it in town," the doctor said soberly and sipped the black coffee she'd poured. "Terrible. Downright deplorable. Men have differences, there are courts of law."

She poured coffee for herself and cut a piece of pie for the doctor. "The marshal was here at noon," she said and sat across from him. "He came to arrest Handy."

"Arrest Handy!" The doctor scowled over his glasses. "Whatever for?"

"He thought Handy had a part in that horror," she said and her voice felt small.

"That's ridiculous!" the doctor said angrily and stood. "Handy could no more take part in such a massacre than I. I'll see the marshal and find out what's behind this."

"Sit down, Doctor." His reaction was unexpected. "He didn't take Handy to jail."

The doctor sighed and sat down again to his pie and coffee. "How in the world did he connect Handy with the killings?"

"A herder had seen a shoot-out between Handy and a sheep guard the day before," she said solemnly. "He escaped the raiders. He thought Handy had killed the guard and described Handy to the marshal, who found out who he was and assumed he'd been with the men who killed the others and the sheep. The guard had fired at Handy first, on our property, and Handy had scarcely wounded him. He brought him here alive." Bitterly, she added, "Jake killed the man later. Handy was here the night of the killings. I know because I saw him."

"I don't think Handy ever would fire the first shot," the doctor said thoughtfully.

"I don't know," she said miserably. "They say he's a gunman."

"Who says that?" the doctor asked impatiently.

"Jake," she said and swallowed the lump in her throat. "He said Pa knew it, too, and that's why he kept Handy on, to be here to kill if there's trouble with the sheepmen."

"I wouldn't take Jake's word for the weather if it was raining," the doctor said disgustedly. "Did you ask your Pa about Handy?"

"No," she said and looked into her cup. "I didn't need to. There are too many other things. He always wears a gun, not like other men do, tied so he can draw it fast."

"I've noticed that," the doctor agreed, "but men have their peculiarities about their guns. They're very personal. There may have been a time in Handy's past when he felt it was necessary to always be armed. He certainly needed a gun when he was attacked and scalped by the Indians."

"Yes," she said, "but he doesn't just wear a gun. Every night he practices shooting, with a pistol and with a rifle. Guns are the only thing that interest him. He even gave me a derringer. I can't imagine how he came by it unless he stole it."

"Practices?" the doctor asked and chuckled. "At the old target wheel by the haystack? I'll bet Jed put him onto that."

The remark startled her. "I hadn't thought of it that way. Pa did, soon as Handy was on his feet. Pa gave him the gun and rifle, too. He said it would give him something to do to pass the time until he was well enough to work."

"Well, you see then," the doctor said patiently, "his shooting at the target doesn't indicate he's a gunman."

Nan bit her lip. "Maybe Pa did it because he knew he was."

"There's one way to settle that," the doctor said briskly. "Forget these things that make you doubt and just come right out and ask your Pa if he is."

"It's not only that, although being a gunman and a killer is the worst." She felt wretched. "He goes to town and drinks and gambles with my brothers, and whatever else they do. They're bad enough by themselves. They make Pa's heart ache and he can't do a thing with them. Now they've got Handy to lead them on."

"That's nonsense, Nan," the doctor said sharply. "I'd have heard of it if there'd been such goings-on. I know about your brothers. I'm dead certain Handy is no such scoundrel. Who carried a tale like that to you?"

"It wasn't just what Jake told me." The words were beginning to choke her. "I saw him come home one night with my brothers. They were so drunk they couldn't ride and Handy staggered when he carried them into the bunkhouse."

"Even as strong a man as Handy would stagger under the load of your beefy brothers," the doctor said and smiled. "It appears to me Jake has gone considerable out of his way to give Handy a black character. What does Handy have to say for himself?"

"I haven't spoken to him since I found out all about him," she said. "It wouldn't do any good. He'd just deny everything."

"It isn't like you, Nan, to be unreasonable," he said softly. "A man has a right to give his side."

"I won't listen to him," she said stubbornly. "I don't want to discover he's a liar on top of all else."

The doctor looked sternly at her. "Then ask your Pa and your brothers."

"I can't," she said. "I'd be ashamed to admit I'd been interested in such a man."

"Bah! You're afraid you'll find out that you've been wrong."

"I'm afraid I'll find out I'm right." She blinked away the tears that came without warning. "I'd be happy if I were wrong but I'd be even more pained than I am now. I could never face him again, not after the way I've treated him."

"If you simply told him you were sorry, I think he'd be so happy he'd never question why."

"I just couldn't ask Pa and my brothers and I can't bring myself to say anything to Handy."

"I think you'd find it worth your effort," the doctor said and finished his pie. "In my opinion Handy is honest and upstanding. He has courage and he's a gentleman. He's no gunman and neither a drunkard nor a gambler. He deserves a hearing." He pushed his chair back and stood. "I'd best be getting on."

At the door, she could not hold back her tears. "Oh, Doctor," she cried. "What am I going to do?"

"Do what your heart tells you," he said gently.

She stood on the porch and watched him drive away. She could not bring herself to do the things the doctor had suggested but she felt better that she'd talked with him. It was confusing. All they'd done was to talk about Handy.

◎◎◎◎◎◎◎◎◎◎◎◎◎

# CHAPTER XX

◎◎◎◎◎◎◎◎◎◎◎◎◎

Jake was roaring drunk when he returned to headquarters that Sunday night. Handy was sitting on the bunkhouse stoop enjoying a smoke and the evening. The moon was big and full and spilled silvery light over the river and the hills. The air was crisp and fresh. Inside someone was playing a harmonica and a five-handed poker game was in progress. He saw Jake coming down the road canting in his saddle. The range boss did not stop at the barn to unsaddle and turn the buckskin to pasture but rode to the bunkhouse and left the horse standing when he toppled to the ground. He picked himself up and tottered to the stoop.

"Git out of my way, you dam' stinker," he bellowed when he saw Handy.

Handy stepped away from the stoop.

Jake took a rolling step and confronted him. "Had to finish the job you was hired to do and kill that sheep guard for you," he rumbled. "Near got throwed in jail for it. Gonna make you pay for that." He brought up his fist in a roundhouse punch at Handy's jaw.

Handy caught Jake's wrist and threw the arm away. "Take it easy, Jake," he said.

The hands had heard the ruckus. Little Red and some of the others who weren't playing poker were bunched at the doorway.

"Don' tell me what to do, you dam' jelly belly," Jake shouted. "An' keep your paws off me."

"Better get to bed, Jake," Handy said.

"I tol' you, min' your own dam' business." Jake brought up his fist again.

Handy grabbed it and this time held on. "I'll take you on, Jake, any time when you're sober," he said. He tugged Jake up the stoop and pushed him through the scrambling hands. Jake swayed and swore. In the lantern light his turquoise eyes looked as if they had embers in them. He'd drooled and spit edged his beard. Handy went back out and led the buckskin to the barn. He unsaddled it and turned the horse to pasture.

Jake was outside again when Handy returned and half a dozen hands were on the stoop or in the doorway. They weren't talking but they were watching and waiting.

"No-count bastard," the range boss ranted. "No dam' good bastard. Gonna tell the ol' man I fired you." He started stumbling in the direction of the white house.

"In the morning," Handy said. He took Jake by the arm and turned him around.

"I tol' you, don' you put your hands on me," Jake snarled. He brought back his arm to start another wild swing.

"Sorry about this," Handy muttered. "There's no other way." He crashed his fist into Jake's beard and found his jaw. The big man's knees buckled and he crumpled. Handy hoisted him across his shoulder, bending under the burden of the weight. The men gave way and he carried Jake to his room and dropped him on his cot. Jake's lips fluttered and he started to snore. There was silence in the bunkhouse when Handy walked back to the stoop and built another smoke.

Jake was hard-eyed and looked meaner than usual when he stomped into the cook shack the next morning. He was chewing the inside of his cheek and his beard was jumping. The rat-faced ragtail, Little Red, was with him and his eyes were bright.

"Hear I owe you for what you done to me last night," Jake said, low-voiced and menacing.

"Sorry, Jake," Handy said. "You were drunk."

"Damn right I was drunk," Jake yelled. "Only reason you downed me was 'cause I was drunk. I'm warning you, Southern, drunk or sober don't you never put your hand to me again or I'll pound you to pulp before I kill you."

Little Red snickered.

Inside, Handy's bile was bubbling but he clamped his jaw and said nothing. He finished his coffee and started to the kitchen with his dishes.

"No need to saddle up this morning, Southern," Jake called. "Today you clean out the barn."

Jake intended the job he gave him to be degrading, Handy realized. Pitching manure was not distasteful to him but the way Jake had put the spurs to him right from the start was intolerable. Nan seemed resolute in her determination to avoid him. Life at the Lazy J had become insufferable. He considered his indebtedness to Jed would be dispatched when he took up a gun and sided him in the showdown with the sheepmen. He could drift on then. But the hell of it was, he was shackled to the Lazy J until he'd earned enough money to buy a horse and saddle.

The next day Jake put him to digging post holes. It was demeaning to a tophand to be doing sodbuster work.

Jed came to his rescue Wednesday morning. "Come on up here a minute," Jed called from the back door as Handy started into the cook shack.

Handy went to the house hopefully.

"Ride out and see where them snoozers and their stinkers have got to," Jed said and made a dour face. "Must be near to Green River by this time. We got to be ready to parley with them. Or fight."

With the gun belt riding low and the Henry in the boot, jerky and biscuits in a saddlebag and coffee in the canteen, Handy put the mustang to a trot on the road to Green River. It lifted his spirits to be off the Lazy J on this crisp day. He thought he'd take a moment to ask Doc Bainbridge whether he'd had a chance to talk with Nan but first he tied up at the Steer Head saloon on the west end of Main Street and went in for Bull Durham and some lucifers. Two men, shopkeepers, were chatting over beer and he listened idly as he waited for the barkeep to get down to him.

". . . 'pears he means to stay," the stocky one wearing a stained butcher's apron was saying.

"What you say his name was?" the second asked. He wore a black vest and white shirt with a stiff collar but no tie.

"Smathers," the butcher said and blew the suds from his beer.

Handy gave their conversation his intent attention. That was the name of the man the gunman had said owned the sheep.

"Got a big band on the way, you say?" the man in the vest asked.

"So I hear, biggest flock ever come into the territory," the butcher said. "A couple dozen herders and thirty or so riders to guard them. He brought more guards with him when he got the telegram about the killings. That herder that got away had his name wrote down and got the marshal to send it."

"Be good for business with all them new folks here," the second man said with satisfaction.

Handy debated whether to return at once to the Lazy J with this information. The one man with whom the ranchers had to talk was Smathers. On the other hand, it appeared the additional gunmen had been expected because the flock had been held beyond Fort Bridger before the slaughter and the marshal's telegram. It looked as if Smathers had come in prepared to fight. The ranchers would need a show of strength to make him listen. He did not ride back to the ranch or stop at the doc's. Putting his heels to the mustang, he took the trail west at a gallop. He needed to fix the flock's position and verify the number of guns.

He expected to sight the flock nearing the Green River Valley and kept a wary eye for outriders in the distance. It was his intention to veer wide at the haze of dust against the blue and count riders while flattened on a baked hill with the mustang concealed on the slope behind. Now pressed for time, he ate the biscuits and jerky Li Shu had given him and drank cold coffee in the saddle. He reached Fort Bridger before noon without encountering the sheep. Puzzled that the flock should still be holding, he pushed on to the hill where he had watched five days before and stared down on cropped grass where sheep had grazed. The plain was empty. The sheep had disappeared. He bristled, thinking he knew where the sheep had been driven and trotted the horse down to the holding ground. The trail the flock had left was plain and so was the plan. The sheep had been herded upland over the rolling brown hills through an arid area where there were no ranches. By circling beyond the Slash Dot spread, the herders could drive the flock onto the open range from the north, unobserved. With the mustang's nose pointed due north, he ran it hard over the packed earth the five thousand sheep had compacted with their hooves. When the horse began to heave, he'd walk it until it had its wind again, and then he'd gallop on. It was imperative he locate the band and get word back of this maneuver.

A good two hours passed before the hazed sky told him the sheep were trampling the ground ahead. He was west of Church Butte and the flock was some miles ahead. He reined in the horse to let it blow while he watched the sky. The horse was nearly spent and he could not risk pursuit. There was no wind, and now that he was stopped he could see the curtain of dust was hanging northeasterly. The herders had started the circle to the range. The mustang needed a few minutes' rest and Handy built a smoke and swallowed some coffee. The butcher at the saloon had said the sheep guard had been doubled and Handy would have to take his word for it. Only Smathers could stop the outbreak of a range war now.

The mustang was sturdy and ran again when Handy put it toward Church Butte. It was late afternoon and the blazing sun was getting low when Handy pulled up at the back of the house and called, "Jed!"

Nan came to the door. "Pa's in his office."

She did not turn and walk away as she'd done so many times before but he had no time now to talk or plead with her. He climbed out of the saddle, threw down the reins and ran past her.

"What is it, what'd you come across?" Jed asked in quick alarm when Handy clattered into his office.

Handy was breathing hard. "They left the trail. Their intentions are clear. They mean to slip onto the range from the north."

"Damnit!" Jed jumped to his feet. His eyes were icy. "How far they from the range?"

"I put them west of Slash Dot land from what I've heard of it," Handy said.

Jed crashed his fist on the desk. "We got to get the boys together and face them right now."

"That would only start the shooting," Handy said. "What you've got to do is see a man named Smathers. He's the owner of this flock and the sheep that were slaughtered. He's in Green River."

"What the hell we got to see him for?" Jed demanded angrily. "We got to stop them stinking sheep before they get on the range and spoil it."

"They've got their orders," Handy said. "Only man who can stop them is Smathers."

"We'll stop them," Jed said fiercely, "but I'll give this Smathers a chance. We'll go out right now and stop them and leave some of the boys to hold them and then we'll go to talk with Smathers."

"Won't work," Handy asserted. "We'll be outnumbered. Smathers put fifteen more sheep guards on that flock. There are thirty hired guns with them now."

"By God, that does it," Jed exploded. "Is his intention clear to you now? He aims to fight. We'll round up every hand on the Lazy J, and X Bar and Slash Dot can do the same. Come on." He came around his desk, grasped Handy's arm and pulled him along.

Handy did not expect to see Nan but she was still in the kitchen. She looked as if she wanted to say something to him but Jed tugged him out. He looked over his shoulder and Nan was standing in the doorway. He thought she looked forlorn.

"You mean to go out there tonight?" he asked.

Jed grunted. "Can't waste no more time."

"We'll be ambushed," Handy warned. "They'll see or hear us coming and take cover. We'll be mounted and they'll pick us off like crows on a limb."

Jed stopped and looked at Handy. His eyes were piercing. "You're right."

Handy was relieved. "Then you'll ride in tonight and see Smathers?"

"No," Jed said firmly. "We'll make camp tonight on the north end of the open range. We got to see not one more woolly puts its hoof on that grass. When it's daylight and we can see who is what, we'll go out to meet them."

Jed slammed into the cook shack and Handy followed. Roy, Ron and Rod were playing seven-card stud and drinking coffee.

"It's come and they mean to fight," Jed told them. "They're a day from the range and they brought a army of gunmen. Roy, round up Jake and 'bout ten of the hands. Jake'll know the ones can shoot. Them with rifles. Ron, get up to the Slash Dot and tell Gene what's happened. Tell him to get ready with all the guns he can put together. Rod, you do the same at the X Bar. Tell Gene and Ed, wait for us. You two stay with them. We'll camp out and face them when it's light." He looked at Handy. "Get a fresh horse and come back to the house."

While Handy was at the horse pasture saddling another mustang, the brothers came for their horses. They wore gun belts and carried rifles. They seemed to be in high spirits and Roy had exchanged his sulk for a smile. "Going to notch some scallops," he said and laughed.

"I hope it doesn't come to that," Handy said. He cinched up and rode to the house. Jed heard him and called to come in. He was at the table drinking coffee and he wore a gun belt. Nan had said her Pa had sworn he'd never carry a gun again.

"Get a cup from the shelf and help yourself," he said, and when Handy was at the table, "Heard about that ruckus at the bunkhouse the other night. Got the straight of it, how you had to knock Jake flat to get him to bed. He don't thank you for it. Wanted you here so's I could give you a word of warning in private. If there's gunplay, keep a eye on him."

◎◎◎◎◎◎◎◎◎◎◎◎◎

# CHAPTER XXI

◎◎◎◎◎◎◎◎◎◎◎◎◎

The mounts of forty-eight dark riders drummed a war-like cadence as they trotted beside the retreating river in the ghostly moonlight. The armed men in the saddles were for the most part solemn and subdued. Jed, Ed and Gene, and behind them Jake and Handy, were in the vanguard, tight-lipped and straight-backed. Handy had been surprised at how much the X Bar and Slash Dot owners resembled Jed, seasoned like weathered trees that had been buffeted by many a storm. The Lazy J company just behind was in disciplined formation except for its rear guard, which was boisterous. Roy, Ron and Rod nearly fell from their saddles at the jocular sallies they mounted.

"Gonna tan some belts of gunmen pelts," Roy sang and the three hung over their horses' necks and yowled.

"Gonna make hair boots of herders' scalps," Ron boasted and laughter rumbled from all three.

"Gonna line my coat with ten lamb skins," Rod promised and they howled like wolves.

Roy started the litany again. "Gonna shoot sheepdogs like they was hogs."

Jed reined his horse about and trotted it back. "You boys got a bottle?"

"Nope," Roy gurgled. "But we're sure as hell full of spirits." That was hilarious enough for more mirth.

"This ain't no hoedown." The old man's voice pealed on the sharp night air. "Shut your yammering or I'll send you packing."

They quieted some but from time to time a hushed remark from one of them provoked another outburst.

The contingents from the Slash Dot and X Bar followed the Lazy J, each led by its range boss. The men were silently sober. They were cowboys, not soldiers or gunmen, Handy reflected, and they realized the men they'd face were mercenaries. Beside him, Jake loomed in his saddle and did not turn his head or speak a word. Jed's warning echoed in Handy's ears. It was entirely possible the range boss would try to kill him but he did not think Jake would risk a shot except from his back.

It was nearing midnight when the company halted in a shadowy stand of pine and spruce on a high plateau not far from the north boundary of the open range. Three men, one from each outfit, went on ahead another mile to spell each other at guard. The moon was down and the night obscured. The men from the three ranches made no fires before they bedded down. They drank cold coffee, built smokes and rolled up in their blankets.

There were no disturbances during the night and they trooped out at sunup, gray and grim. They ate their biscuits and jerky in their saddles. Ahead, the three captains, Jed, Gene and Ed, exchanged brief words and Jed dropped back between Handy and Jake.

"We'll parley if they'll hold for it," he said, looking straight ahead and not speaking directly to either of them. "Doubt they will."

Jake looked darkly at Handy and growled, "Why? Thing to do is don't give them no chances. Circle them like Indians and first pick off them men on horses."

Handy chilled at the way Jake put it. "And finish the others, the herders, off afterwards?"

Jed said sternly, "We won't kill unless we must. If they agree to hold until Smathers comes out, we'll leave everybody here to keep peace and I'll ride in for him. Doubt much will come of it but we'll give it a go-around." He moved ahead again.

It was as much of a concession as he could hope, Handy thought.

"This your doing, Southern?" Jake asked angrily.

"I mentioned it," Handy said.

Jake looked at him savagely. "Who you think you be? I'm boss here. What you doing, riding up front? Get back with the hands where you belong."

"Not until Jed tells me," Handy said and looked at Jake. He was chewing his cheek. The matted black beard was twitching and the turquoise eyes reflected nothing.

The sun was at high noon when two riders took form in the distance. For a moment they were motionless, in view on the high brown tableland, and then they disappeared.

Jed shifted in his saddle and called to Handy, "They went back. What'll they do?"

He looked at the range boss. Ugly storm clouds had settled on Jake's face. "Bring up their guns," he told Jed.

Jed's face was set and grim. "Pass the word to be ready," he told Handy.

Jake roared the order back at once.

Something like half an hour passed and no riders appeared ahead. The plateau they were riding was broad and flat ahead but there were jumbled hills to the west.

"We'd better watch our flank and rear," Handy warned Jed.

"Pass it back," Jed shouted.

Jake bellowed the order. Hate contorted his dark face when he slitted his opaque eyes at Handy.

Word passed up from the back that riders were coming up behind the group. Handy reined out to have a look and Jake pulled off to the other side. About a mile off a band was pounding toward the cowboys.

"Turn around," Jake thundered.

"Hold it," Handy called.

The men pulled up in confusion and the horses milled.

Jed jerked around. "What the hell, Handy!"

"It's a trap," Handy yelled. "That's only half of them behind us. Another bunch is still ahead. One way or another, they figure to take us from the rear."

Jed didn't hesitate. "Ed, Gene," he called, "take your men and meet them behind. Lazy J will take on the others."

Jake barked, "There's nobody coming on ahead. Southern's yellow. He don't want to fight."

"I'll take his word," Jed fired back. "Come on."

Jed galloped straight on, Jake at one side and Handy on the other. The Lazy J crew followed. The Slash Dot and X Bar men wheeled some thirty-two strong and the men put rifles to their shoulders.

There'd be no parley now, Handy knew.

Shots sang out behind as a line of riders appeared charging toward the Lazy J crew. When the sheep guard came within range, a rifle cracked and Handy saw Jake's Winchester at his shoulder. He was levering rapidly and the gunmen were returning the fire. The cowboys spread out and began to shoot. Handy sighted and fired, sighted and fired and two men tumbled from their saddles. Beside him, Jed had fired four shots and dropped three gunmen. Handy thought Jake had accounted for one. The remaining gunmen still came on and one by one the Lazy J hands picked them off until only unmounted horses fled before them. Handy reined about to count the casualties. Three men were on the ground. He pulled up and jumped out of the saddle, going from one to another. Two were dead. They were Ron and Rod. Roy's shoulder was shattered but he was alive. Handy patched him up as well as he could with bandage rags from a saddlebag and helped him to his horse. At the rear only an occasional shot snapped but ahead a pistol was spitting. Jake was weaving through the fallen gunmen and shooting the wounded.

Handy slung his leg over the mustang and galloped toward Jake but Jed reached the range boss first. Jake had fired three more times and looked pleased with himself.

"Why'd you do that, kill them that wasn't dead?" Jed stormed.

Jake looked surprised. "So's there'd be no witnesses against us," he barked.

The Slash Dot and X Bar outfits came up. Their ranks had been thinned.

"How many?" Jed asked Gene.

"Four X Bar, three Slash Dot," Gene said. "I see two of yours is down."

"Ron and Rod," Jed said gruffly. "Roy is wounded."

Jake broke in, "Come on. We can pick up the bodies later." He was breathing hard and his face was fiercely lighted.

"Where to and what for?" Handy asked.

"Finish the job." Jake curled his lip and showed a tooth. "Like you never do." He started to lift his rifle but Handy's Colt was on him and he lowered the barrel.

"Shove the rifle in the boot and get down," Handy commanded.

"Get that gun off me," Jake shouted and looked at Jed.

The old man's eyes turned frosty and he said nothing.

When Jake was on the ground, Handy said, "Take off your gun belt and hang it on the saddle."

Jed sat his horse and did not interfere. Jake fumed but did as he was ordered. The hands from the three ranches surrounded Jake and Handy in a wide circle for the showdown.

"Take his horse and iron, and mine," Handy told Jed and climbed down. He removed his gun belt, tossed his hat to the side and bared his skull bone. Jake gnawed his cheek and squared off. The air was empty of all sound except for an occasional nicker from a horse.

Handy and Jake moved warily toward each other, both waiting to take advantage of the opponent's first strike. Abruptly, Jake closed in, guard up, big fist cocked, and hooked Handy's ankle with his boot toe. Handy sprawled and Jake leaped to crush him just as Handy rolled aside and sprang to his feet. Jake balled over and came up fast. Handy rushed him before he had his balance and rocked him with a smashing blow to the jaw. Jake drove his fist into Handy's gut and he grunted at the pain.

They both crouched, backing off and side-stepping. Jake reached out with a left that grazed Handy's temple and a right uppercut that scraped his jaw. The blows hurt but did no great damage. Handy got through the opening with a sledge-hammer right to Jake's nose that made blood spurt. He followed immediately with a left and right to the nose and felt the bones crunch.

Jake bellowed like a stuck steer and rushed, butting Handy's midsection with his head and knocking out his wind. Handy backed away with his guard up and kept out of reach until he could breathe again. Blood from Jake's broken nose was splattered over his face and shirt. He charged again head down. Handy jumped aside and clubbed the back of Jake's neck. He went down and Handy waited until the range boss was on his feet again to close in with a short right-left-right combination to the jaw. Jake staggered Handy with a right smash to the midsection.

Handy backed off to catch his breath. His belly was aching but otherwise he felt strong and even exhilarated.

Jake had been hurt and his eyes blazed. He rushed in swinging wildly and clobbered Handy with blows to the eye and temple that stunned him. He put his fists to his face and Jake hammered his midsection. Handy felt blood running down his cheekbone. He caught Jake with a short right uppercut that drove him back. Handy followed quickly with left and right uppercuts and a left jab to the throat that brought blood gurgling from Jake's mouth. He backed away hacking and spewing blood over his beard.

Handy closed in, smashing at Jake's chin. The bearded one's lips were puffed and his left eye was swelling shut. He went for Handy's midsection with a right that didn't have much behind it and tried to wrap his arms around him in a bear hug. Handy backed away and Jake tried to crack Handy's groin with his knee.

With Jake off balance, Handy closed in for the kill. He doubled Jake with a left to the belly and felled him with a crashing uppercut to the jaw that cracked bone. Jake sprawled on the ground and did not move. His face was a pulpy mash of blood. Handy's midsection was tender and one side of his face was swollen and bleeding. He swiped his cheek, picked up his hat, dusted it on his shrunken rump and sloshed it on. The hands cheered riotously.

"Guess I'll be drifting on," Handy told Jake. He knew he was through at the Lazy J but he felt good, better than he had in a long, long while. "All right with you if I leave the horse at the livery stable in Green River?"

"Now what the hell you mouthing about?" Jed bawled. He jerked his head in the direction of Jake, who was pushing himself to rubbery legs. "He's the one that's done, not you."

Jake's usually stony eyes were glassy when he screwed his head around the circle of cowboys whose cheers for Handy now changed to hoots at the former range boss. With his jaw hanging loose, broken nose still spilling blood, and closed eye, he stumbled to his buckskin and managed to throw a leg over the saddle the third time he tried.

Jed gave him his gun and rifle. He pulled a pouch from his Levis and tossed it to Jake. He missed the throw. Scornfully, Jed said, "There's two double eagles and some silver. That ought to cover the salary I owe and whatever you're leaving behind including the roan. It'll save you the shame of facing the boys if you came to the office for your pay."

Jake looked purely pained when he pulled a boot from the stirrup and dragged a leg over the saddle. It was a mighty effort for him to bend down in front of the hands from the three ranches and pick up the poke. He held the horn of the saddle in both hands with bleeding knuckles and pulled himself up on the first try. The cow pokes broke rank and Big Jake rode west without a word, if he could still speak, and without a backward look.

# CHAPTER XXII

It had been a costly battle with the invading sheep forces and the toll on both sides was sobering.

"I'm sorry about Ron and Rod," Handy said simply when he'd buckled on his gun belt and climbed back into the saddle. "The others, too, and Roy's smashed shoulder."

"The boys wasn't worth much but they was mine," Jed said. "You was right, son. You was right. We should of tried the other way."

"It isn't over yet," Handy pointed out. "We have that big flock of sheep on our hands, and the herders and wagons. Now you've got to talk with Smathers and see what can be worked out."

Gene and Ed reined beside Jed and Handy again. Their faces were grim.

"What now?" Gene asked Jed.

Jed breathed heavily. He looked drawn and his face seemed to have more wrinkles in it than usual. He said, "You and Ed each take half your crews and get on back. I'll take half what's left of mine. Leave the others here with one of your foremen to hold the sheep and clean up the battlefield. I'll take Handy and go in to talk with this Smathers. After what's happened, he'll think twice before bringing in more guns. We'll convince him to ride out here and order his foreman to trail them woollies back to Oregon." He turned to Handy. "Suit you, son?"

"I don't know," Handy said thoughtfully. "There'll be other flocks and more killings unless we can work out some compromise that both the ranchers and sheepmen will find agreeable. I'd say figure out the number of cattle and sheep the range will accommodate and divide it up that way, fence off part for the sheep and keep them on their side, off cow grass. Get the government to recognize what's been done and make the agreement stick."

Ed frowned and objected, "It'll hold down the head of cows we run."

Handy shook his head. "If you don't do something like it, the sheepmen will try to take over the entire range with their big flocks and you'll have nothing."

"I think your man's right," Gene told Jed.

"So do I, much as I hate the snoozers and their stinkers," Jed agreed. "I should of listened to him before when he tried to tell me."

The three ranchers with their dead and wounded began the procession back to their headquarters. At the river, the Lazy J parted with the other outfits and crossed to the open public domain above Jed's north range. Roy rode with Jed and Handy. His face was pale and he seemed in pain from his shoulder.

They were on Lazy J land before he spoke. "We been wrong, Pa, Ron and Rod was, and me. Took Handy here to straighten out my thinking. Not that he ever said a word about things to me. He just showed by what he done. Gonna miss them two brothers but we was headed wrong. Gonna set things right. Work like the other hands and just go to town Saturdays."

Jed looked at his son a moment. His eyes were not so cold as usual. He said, "That's good, Roy. Move your war bag back in your bedroom in the house."

"Not until I earn it, Pa," Roy said.

Jed nodded his head and said, "You'll have a fair judge of that." He swung to Handy. "You're the range boss now."

Handy's heart lifted and then fell with a thud. He'd thought immediately that now he could ask Nan to marry him but he'd remembered just as quickly how she'd turned on him. "I'm obliged, Jed," he said. "I'll do my best, but I won't run the crew with angry words and an iron fist like Jake."

"That's why you're boss," Jed said. "You got more gravel in

your craw than any man I ever saw but you're honest and just and I'm proud to have you run the spread."

Roy said, "I'm glad you done that, Pa."

"That's good, too, Roy," Jed said. "One day you and Handy will run the ranch." To Handy he said, "Your salary is doubled and you get a cut on what we sell. There's a piece of land on the river, above the fishing hole Nan favors, would take a cabin if you'd a mind to buy it. Sell it outright for twenty-five dollars and the boys could pitch in when it's slow and help you raise it. Range boss needn't to live with the crew."

"I'd like to buy it and build the cabin," Handy said and thought dismally of the deteriorated relationship with Nan.

They were leaving the north range and nearing the headquarters. Jed turned to Roy again. "Handy and me'll go right on. I'll send the doc out to tend your shoulder. You're looking faint and not up to the ride. You'll have to break the news to Nan about Ron and Rod. Confess I'm not up to facing her. We'll not be back until we've got this settled."

Handy gulped and managed to say, "Ask Nan if she'll favor me with a moment when we return."

Roy smiled faintly and Jed chuckled despite his sorrow but neither made a comment. The crew, with Ron's and Rod's bodies tied on their saddles, followed Roy when Jed and Handy cut off the Lazy J to the road.

"I'm going to let you handle this with Smathers," Jed said as they approached Green River. "It's likely to be a rough go-around and I'd of never trusted it to Jake but I believe you can do it. I'll back you in whatever you lay out to him."

"Couldn't ask for more," Handy mentioned absently. He should have been elated at the unexpected turn of events but he felt downcast. Maybe time would ease the friction that had developed between Nan and him, although she'd been so adamant in her refusal to discuss the circumstances with him, he held little hope.

They tied up first at Doc Bainbridge's and Handy went into the office with Jed. He meant to learn whether the doc had talked with Nan and if he hadn't to ask him to try and have a word with her after he'd fixed Roy's shoulder.

The doc shook his head gravely at news of the battle. "It's too bad about the boys," he told Jed. "There's been too much killing. Isn't there some other way?"

"Handy maybe come up with a answer," Jed said. "We're going to see that sheepman Smathers now."

Handy stepped back into the office when Jed walked out. "Be with you in a minute," he called and quickly asked the doctor, "Have the chance to talk with Nan?"

The doc examined Handy over the tops of his spectacles and smiled. "I think there's hope. Jake and maybe the boys had given her some peculiar notions about you. She was disappointed and hurt at what they said you were but she wants to believe you. I think she'll listen to you now."

It was the best news Handy'd had in days. "Thanks, Doc, that's all I wanted to hear," he shouted and ran out.

They found the sheepman eating a beefsteak at a table by himself in the big, bare dining room at the Territorial Hotel. He was squinty-eyed and shrunken but he wore a gun belt and, the way his hand dropped, looked ready to use it. "If I ask you to set, you'll spoil my dinner," he said and chewed the words as if they were lemons when Jed told him who they were. "But set and tell me what's happened. I know things was shaping up to a showdown."

They pulled out chairs and ordered coffee from a frumpy girl who eyed them suspiciously. Handy said, "We didn't come to argue, Smathers. We came to see whether we couldn't find some way out of the range war. It was you brought in hired guns. We went out this morning to talk but they tried to trap us in cross fire. Your guns all are dead. We lost nine. This feud has to end."

Smathers paled. Angrily, he demanded, "The sheep and herders? You clubbed them like you did my other outfits."

"No," Handy said evenly. He expected the little man to call him out. "We left a small crew to keep order while we came in to talk with you. Our intention was to take you out and have you order the sheep driven back but that'd just be asking for more trouble. We don't want that if it can be avoided. You know as well as we that it's no good putting cows and sheep on the same graze. A cow will eat after a horse but neither horse nor cow will eat after sheep."

Smathers' eyes were blazing. "What are you trying to tell me?"

"We'll meet you halfway," Handy said. "If you're willing to fence off the part of the range where you run sheep, we'll work out a division of the public land that's fair to both interests. We'll talk to the politicians and officials and work it out with them."

"I got as much right to that range as anybody," Smathers said defiantly.

"I'm afraid not," Handy said patiently. "We've established grazing rights over the years. You can't just move in and drive our cows off. The officials know our position. They don't want a range war any more than we do, but if it comes to a battle there are a lot more cattlemen than sheepmen and the officials will sympathize with us. I don't know who was behind the attack on the three camps you had on the range. I heard the raiders were masked. I don't hold with what they did but it should show you what the feeling is, that and the fight this morning. Come to terms, Smathers, or both you and we will suffer."

Smathers' eyes shifted from Handy to Jed and he gnawed at a corner of his lip. Finally he said, "I don't want to hire another batch of gunslingers and I can't afford to risk them sheep. How you aim to handle it?"

"Hold your flock where it is while we settle what's your pasture and what's ours and build your fence," Handy said. "That range may be public land but when the officials hear what is being done they'll not waste time. Only change in matters is there will be one piece public for sheep and one piece public for cattle."

"Dunno," Smathers said. "Can't say I like it but got no choice. What you want me to do?"

"Get out there and tell your foreman what we're doing," Handy said. "Get your men started on the fence as soon as we've agreed where it's to be. We'll send whatever men you need to help."

Jed spoke up. "It's not everything but it's a start. We got to learn to live with each other. I'll go out to the woollies with Smathers and stop for a talk with Gene and Ed. You get back to the Lazy J, Handy. From what you asked Roy, I think you and Nan got some overdue talking to make."

◎◎◎◎◎◎◎◎◎◎◎◎◎

# CHAPTER XXIII

◎◎◎◎◎◎◎◎◎◎◎◎◎◎◎

Handy trotted the tired mustang down the autumn-browned slope toward the ranch house in the blaze of the afternoon sun that so burnished the sky it seemed the blue had turned to white. Half-blinded, he hopefully and nervously searched the porch for Nan but did not find her. After the doctor's encouragement and Jed's remark about an overdue conversation, he was disturbed she wasn't there and turned the horse's head toward the corral when he heard her voice calling his name. At that moment a shaft of sunshine slanted through the house from the back door and he discovered Nan standing in the front doorway touched by a golden aura. She was the most beautiful picture he'd ever seen.

He vaulted from the saddle and ran toward the porch calling, "Nan, Nan, Nan."

She came to meet him with her hands held out. Her gentle eyes had tears in them. She was softly repeating his name again and again as he had hers. Then she was in his arms and he was kissing lips that were sweet with warmth and promise. It was more than he'd ever dreamed or hoped.

"I'm sorry about your brothers," he said gently when he wiped away her tears with the corner of the beige kerchief he'd given her and she'd never worn before. Today it was tucked into the open neck of a brown, light shirt.

"So am I," she said and sniffed, "but the tears are for you, not them. Oh, Handy, can you ever forgive me for making you so miserable?"

He held her close and kissed her once again. "There's nothing to forgive."

"I doubted you," she said wretchedly and clung to him.

"You must have had your reasons," he said quietly. "They aren't important now."

"They are," she murmured. "I finally came to my senses. I tried to tell you yesterday but there was such urgency in the air and Pa wouldn't let me talk to you."

"I know, Nan." A calmness had come over him he had not known in weeks.

"I thought you were leading my brothers on, drinking and gambling, and worst of all that you were a gunman." She choked back a sob that started and after a moment said, "I knew in my heart it couldn't be so. Then today Roy told me all you'd done for him, and Ron and Rod—how you'd stood by them, fought for them, brought them home when they couldn't even ride, after the way they'd been treating you. And how it was you who'd tried every way you could to prevent that awful battle this morning."

"Please, Nan, it's over now," he said and stroked her hair. "I love you."

She clutched him tightly and said breathlessly, "I love you, Handy."

"That's all that counts." Abruptly, he stepped back, holding her hands and smiling. "Wait here. I'll be right back. I have a surprise for you."

"Don't be long, even for a surprise," she pleaded. "We missed so much time we could have been together."

He left the mustang where it was standing and ran to the bunkhouse. Half a dozen of the hands who'd returned from combat were resting on their bunks. Some half rose guiltily but he waved them down and did not disturb them. They watched curiously as he took the golden hairpiece from a kerchief in his Levis and fitted it to his head.

"We'll clean out Jake's old room for you, boss," Little Red called in a piping voice that sounded wheedling.

"That's not for me," he called back and laughed. "When the others get back, all of you can high-card for it."

"Where you going to bunk, boss?" Another wanted to know. "Going to move back to the white house?"

"Nope." He hung his gun belt on a peg. "I'll be moving to the honeymoon cottage."

He left them baffled and ran to the porch, bareheaded, with the hair streaming over his shoulders.

"Oh! What a wonderful surprise!" Nan exclaimed and laughed delightedly when she saw her hair atop his head. "With your bruised and battered face you look like a fallen angel."

He'd forgotten his battle scars. "This isn't the surprise but I do wear it only for special occasions."

"What is the surprise?" she asked and her eyes danced with the pleasure of anticipation.

"We're going for a walk," he said and took her hand.

"Like we used to do. You remembered."

He laughed. "The walk isn't the surprise either. I'm just leading up to it."

"Well, please hurry," she said with sweet impatience.

Hand in hand they wandered through the crisp-leafed cottonwood trees behind the house and along the trickle of water in the river. His heart was filled with the warmth of love and Nan danced at his side.

"The last time we walked here, I had to slow my steps for you," she said. "If next year is normal, the river will be back to the banks and this is a lovely place for a walk at sunset."

"Where is your fishing pool?" he asked.

"Oh yes," she said happily. "You remembered that, too. There would be water there, even now, from the springs."

"Please lead me to the knoll above it."

"All right," she said but she looked startled.

The knoll was a grassy plat that sloped gently to a sandy beach and across the stream a calm pool that looked dark green and deep. Alder hedged it and back on the knoll three great cottonwood trees embraced a private, restful park.

He led her to the shade of one of the rustling trees and pulled her to the grass with his arm around her. "Can't you imagine a cozy cabin here, under the trees, with a porch where you could sit in the summer and look out across the river to your pool?"

Her gasp was filled with amazement and she asked in a hushed voice, "How did you know? I've always wanted a cabin here."

Handy chuckled and his arm tightened around her waist. "I suspected as much when I started to fit the pieces together."

"I don't understand," she said very quietly.

Abruptly, he said, "How would you like to be married to the range boss?"

She drew away from him with a little shudder and said disbelievingly, "Jake?"

He laughed and pulled her back. "Didn't Roy tell you anything?"

"Only what I told you," she said, a trifle impatiently. "Why are you teasing me?"

"I'm not teasing, my dear Nan," he said quietly. "I'm the new range boss."

"Handy!" she cried and drew away. She was laughing with tears in her eyes. She wrapped him in her arms and laid her cheek on his chest. "This is the surprise, and the knoll and the cabin. Oh, yes, Handy. Oh, my dear!" And she cried silently.

He held her close and told her, "Your Pa had a hand in all this although I didn't realize it until just now. I'm buying this piece of ground from him. I didn't know what it meant to you but he must have."

She sat away, giggling. "Pa always wanted to be Grandpa." She came closer. "How is it possible for such a sorrowful day to be so filled with happiness?"